SILVER
REPETITION

SILVER
REPETITION

A NOVEL

LILY WANG

NEW YORK
LONDON

Requests for permission to reproduce selections from this book should be
made through our website: https://thenewpress.com/contact.

The excerpt from *Repetition* and *Philosophical Crumbs* by Søren
Kierkegaard on page vii is reproduced with permission of Oxford
Publishing Limited through PLSclear.

Originally published in Canada by House of Anansi Press Inc., 2024
This edition published in the United States by The New Press,
New York, 2024
Distributed by Two Rivers Distribution

ISBN 978-1-62097-856-6 (pb)
ISBN 978-1-62097-861-0 (ebook)
CIP data is available

The New Press publishes books that promote and enrich public
discussion and understanding of the issues vital to our democracy and
to a more equitable world. These books are made possible by the
enthusiasm of our readers; the support of a committed group of
donors, large and small; the collaboration of our many partners in the
independent media and the not-for-profit sector; booksellers, who often
hand-sell New Press books; librarians; and above all by our authors.

www.thenewpress.com

Book design and composition by Lucia Kim

Printed in the United States of America

10 9 8 7 6 5 4 3 2 1

For my mom

I can circumnavigate myself,
but I cannot get beyond myself.
—Søren Kierkegaard

SILVER
REPETITION

part 01

"THIS IS COOL," I say, because no one's speaking.

"I brought you here so you would think I'm a cool guy."

We are in the Poetry Jazz Café. A young Muhammad Ali collapses against the wall behind the bar. Before us, a crowd, swaying along with the projection, shadows continuing their side-to-side movement with each loop of light. My date introduces me to his friend's girlfriend. He tells me she just returned from Australia and is visiting her boyfriend, a musician whom we are here to watch. She holds her drink with four fingers blocking the label, the smooth ovals of her nails blushing under the subtle light. Her breath like mandarin oranges is the only one I can smell.

"He plays the trumpet," my date leans in to tell me.

My date paid the cover. His name is Johnny.

The Australian girlfriend gives me a polite look before scanning the stage. During the day, the bar is shut to the public, situated between used-clothing stores with open fronts where construction vests hang like a slant of neon lanterns. People wander in the middle of the road, manoeuvring their baby strollers around parked cars and broken pieces of pavement. It's quiet the way weekday afternoons are, when you can hear the puddles and the phone conversations and the *clud-clud* of skateboard wheels.

The deliberate atmosphere inside the café is the sharp purple of dreams, smoke-lit and narrow, swathed in silhouettes. Onstage, the lower half of his body obscured by the crowd, a rapper is chuckling; his mouth floats like a crescent on the surface of a lake. He could be singing or talking. The performance does not register as music to me. Johnny's friend Erik stands behind the rapper, off to the left. I catch glimpses of gold as an offbeat and attractive sound furls from the brass. He plays unaware, he tests notes, he exchanges tender glances with the other members of his band. Candles flicker on darkened hardwood, melting onto silver dishes, warming our faces. It might all be music.

I don't look at Johnny much because he is handsome, which annoys me. He has a serious mouth, full lips, crooked bottom teeth. When no one's watching, I wipe the stamp from my hand and drink from Johnny's glass. I didn't have any ID to prove my age. Johnny smiles and asks to try my ginger beer.

Erik wrote a poem about Johnny's legs. That's how the

two met. Johnny and Erik were at a bar high on cocaine once, and Erik had to get Johnny out of a fight. I must have made a face at "cocaine," because Johnny says, "It's part of the story, just listen." He likes his stories. I tell him I'm not a spy. He tells me he kissed Erik.

There is an interlude. Erik steps down from stage, exchanges a few words with his band, and takes off his toque. He walks over to us and Johnny introduces me as his friend. Again, I feel the girlfriend's polite gaze on me. I tell Johnny's friends that I've never been to the bar before. Erik unrolls the hem of his toque and rolls it back up, scrunching the orange wool in his hands. He pulls his girlfriend in for a kiss. Oranges, mandarins. Johnny and I say our goodbyes and leave in a yellow cab.

Johnny and I had gone on three dates before he called it off. That was about a week ago. I didn't know the first date was meant to be romantic. I hadn't been sure. I don't know what tonight is supposed to be, but I'm glad to be here. I'm glad Johnny texted. I'm glad we're giving it another shot.

In the taxi, the driver's silent presence makes both Johnny and me nervous. Light clumps on the oily glass.

"It's not nice to talk to me about kissing," I say, once we're out of the cab.

I show Johnny the text he sent me, the one about kissing. I remind him he rejected me.

Johnny stretches his neck. "I lost interest for an hour."

We walk across his driveway below a cloudless sky. Johnny steers me from the front of the house to a side stairwell. He reaches over my head and pulls on a screen door—black mesh passing through the night air before my face—and pushes open the door behind it. Everyone I know is settling into basement apartments. I keep finding myself at friends' basement parties, turning my nose from wall to wall, peering down slender-necked vases full of artificial lilies, spring just beyond my view. While I envy their independence, coating those feelings of envy is the stale yellow pollen left over from childhood. Summers spent sitting on the landlord's porch steps until their returning van plugged out the light, sometimes crawling up to their living room from the shared laundry, stretching our weary bodies across their cobalt couch. We laid our underwear across their floorboards to dry, so drunk on sunlight, my parents' faces would glow bright red. My mom, more than any of us, thirsted for light. She would sit at the top of our basement steps with the door cracked open, one hand at the base of her pregnant belly. "Move, you're blocking the way." Our landlord said those cruel words to her. It was rare for the landlord's entire family of five to be gone, and they always had dirty laundry that needed to be washed. My mom pulled up a chair and sat by the only window in our basement apartment, sat until snow caved her in, a ring of blue around the base of the house. When we moved her chair, there were four rings hollowed into the carpet.

Two more doors face us once we're inside. Johnny gestures with slender fingers: one for his place and one for the laundry. I leave my boots by Johnny's bike, kept vertically against the wall to conserve space, and let him lead the way into his living room. His basement is brighter than the one in my memory but just as yellow; time colours memory's movement through me like water touching metal.

Johnny sits me down on his couch. I run my hands against the coarse threading of the cushions, studying the texture as a way to ward off my melancholy. I give each seat cushion a pat, counting three in total. The slipcover is orange-brown with flat felled seams, and despite its worn appearance, the couch gives off no smell. In fact, the basement apartment as a whole carries no scent, not a single spore in the air. Unsure of what to say, I keep my eyes focused on the patchwork cover, offering a compliment about the stitching. Johnny brags to me about not having any roommates. He disappears into his bedroom and returns holding a banjo. He pulls up a stool and takes a seat in front of me. I watch him strumming; a strand of hair falls between his brows. He knows a few chords but not enough for a song. Still, it is the most romantic gesture he's made yet. After three or four tunes, Johnny twirls the head of his banjo with one hand and gives the strings a slap. "You haven't seen my room," he says.

The flooring in Johnny's bedroom is the same as in his living room, washroom, and laundry. His bed frame takes up most of the space on the floor, his bedsheets a flowing chasm of white beneath the plain walls. Above his bed, cinched across a small window, is a piece of cloth evidently cut from the end of another curtain. Johnny changes with the light off. When he finishes, he hands me a clean shirt from his closet so that I can change as well.

Mid-sleep, I open my eyes and find Johnny's back turned to me. I raise my arm and his shadow grows another limb.

Johnny doesn't wake until late afternoon the next day. I don't use my phone for fear of draining its battery. There is nowhere to explore. I pull a wooden crate from beneath Johnny's desk and flip through his collection of vinyl, knowing there's not a single name I'll recognize. I lose interest quickly and return the crate to its spot. Standing up, I spot the olive handle of a stiletto blade. The blade is over three inches long, slender, tapered to a needle-like point. It serves no purpose on the scattered desk. Something like pity moves me to clean up the cheap pencils next to the blade. I linger for a while after by the bedroom door, pencils in hand, wanting to press my face against the door like it's a satin pillow or breastbone.

When Johnny finally emerges, he isn't at all surprised to find me reading his book on his couch. I lift up the Salinger. He says he hasn't touched that one yet. I watch him do his laundry, sleepwalking in and out of his room with a white basket, the soft plastic sides flexing like cartilage.

In the story I'm reading, a man goes down to the beach for

some suntanning, then he goes back into his room and takes out a handgun. There is a girl at the beginning of the story, but then she isn't mentioned again. I read this story once before and had retained no memory of the girl. Reading it again, I feel like it's two stories. When the hunger is unbearable, I leave.

I feel like crying on the streetcar, but I am not alone. When I am home, the urge is gone.

Johnny apologizes over text. It takes him two days to think of me.

In those two days, I gather all the leaves in my backyard into large brown paper bags and move them to the front curb for pickup. Raking is more work than I thought. By this time of year, the leaves have mostly decomposed; what's left has become matted and stringy, hard to clean off the tines. Each time I bring the rake up to the bag, I need to use one hand to steady the handle and the other to brush off the leaves and twigs. I give up on the rake and use both arms to gather the piles, rushing at the ground and hugging it, covering myself in dirt.

There is a smoke tree in my parents' backyard, so most of what I collect is fluff. Come summertime the tree is covered in oval leaves of gold and green. It blooms, and slight winds carry the frothy, purple-burgundy clusters across our deck like dust. I can spend entire mornings just watching the tree sway.

The clusters turn lighter in the fall. Sometimes yellow, translucent, in the rain.

Johnny texts me, "I had a dream about a coffee shop in Leslieville. Do you want to go there with me this week?"

Our tree is dying. I tear the first bag when I try to close it; a twig springs loose and snags my skin.

I ask him, "When?"

The leaves around the base of the tree, the shrubs, I don't touch. They will serve as mulch. Somehow the backyard feels smaller now, exposed.

I envision Johnny on the night he first called, before he changed his mind, then changed it back again. We were cutting across campus, and we both had our hands in our pockets. There was tension in my neck and shoulders, but Johnny was relaxed; he had a serene look to him as he guided me with his elbow. I trod alongside him, so cold that I couldn't stop speaking. That's when I saw the overhead street lamps. White sparks were blooming beneath the lamps' oval covers. Even as we crossed the intersection, I looked back and up at them—those sparks of snow under the orange glow.

"Look!" I kept saying.

✵

Johnny meets me on the station platform downtown and we walk to the streetcar together with our hands in our pockets, sharing the sidewalk. He's in a good mood today. Every few minutes, he jerks one hand out to gesture at something before stuffing it back where it's warm. My eyes follow his swinging arm to the trees. Bean pods dangling from the branches. Long black pods like mummified cocoons. I feel like all my hair could fall. Johnny makes a joke that I miss about the neighbourhood. The streets mostly look the same to me; some are just dirtier than others.

We think the coffee shop has closed down because the lights are off and there are stools stacked against the window, but when we step closer, we can see many people inside, in lines and in the seats, hanging their jackets on black wall hooks or draping them over armrests. Newspapers lie open on round tables, next to cups, plates, and little spoons for stirring. Upon our arrival—marked by a tinkling bell above the door—we are instantly greeted by the warm smell of espresso, sweet fig, chocolate shavings, orange peels drying in spirals, and other such ribboning scents. Bicolour croissants, topped with freshly whipped butter and flaky salt, rest above a display case. When it's our turn to order, Johnny steps forward and touches hands with the barista.

"I didn't know if you'd be in today," Johnny says. He orders two coffees. "Friend from high school," he tells me after.

We take a seat by the entrance, facing the street. From the window, I see people step off the streetcar, holding on to their scarves and looking left and right before crossing the street. Johnny adds sugar to his coffee then mine, tearing the corners off each single-serve before tilting the packs over our mugs together. He places the empty packs, two for each of us, on his saucer. He presses the tip of his finger on a stray sugar crystal and edges it off the table. I am struck by Johnny's indifference and begin to feel the mistake I'm making. Sitting across from Johnny on an antique seat with fringed throws, ornate and flowery. Even my porcelain mug has been rubbed to a shine! I feel myself as I really am, an acquaintance.

I hear the bell tinkle again and again as more people walk in. I excuse myself to use the washroom and must hold onto the railing during my descent. The basement, which seems to be shared with the establishment next door, bears no resemblance to the café upstairs. The toilet is low to the ground and crooked; I have to crouch close to the unclean tiles, many of which are chipped and sound hollow beneath my heels. I stand before the dimly lit mirror, tucking the front end of my shirt into my jeans. The sink is so shallow, it is like a bar of soap that has only been used on one side. I wet my hands to style my hair, slicking any loose strands back with my fingers before heading up. Even now, in the dim light, my hair sparkles from the snow on that first night.

When I get back to the table, I say, "How do I know you like me if you don't hold my hand?"

"You want to hold my hand?" Johnny laughs and offers me what I desire most.

02

THERE IS A DOWNPOUR during the night. I sleep heavily, and if I dream, I do not remember.

I wake to the most orange sky. There is only horizon or no horizon. I put on yesterday's pants and a new sweater, listening to the quiet unreality of rain. Giant peonies glimmer across the sky—with a wave of a sash, the tones change—dream salmon, saucer peony, the houses lined up side by side beneath those ever-drifting petals, white shutters shaking like rabbits in a snow country.

The bus stop is located relatively close to our house, but I cut across the lawn anyway. Blades of grass cling to my boots like tiny-winged insects; intending to rinse my boots off in the gutter, I step down from the curb only to scramble back when I see the bus arriving. Late, the driver does not return my half smile.

A call comes as I'm putting my earbuds in. I press my hand against my bag as the bus makes a long turn, all my weight shifting to the left. Since the number I'm using first belonged to my mom, every once in a while, someone will call speaking Mandarin. But this time it is English that greets me, wraps me in plain yarn, anticipates me. A girl speaks from the other side, and I am so unused to being addressed, it's like I've taken a step back from language. I ask the girl for her name, or she tells me her name without my asking, or while I'm asking. I'm too stunned to retrace the order of our words. She is M. She is not as young as her disembodied voice sounds, her frequency altered by the electromagnetic spectrum. As the bus moves, sound unravels, handled by a succession of cell towers. I hear M's words but only see the hexagon her sound makes. "We saw you with Johnny." She pauses. "How are you?"

The last time I saw M, she was sitting in a tub with three other girls. There were girls barefoot on the washroom floor, a picket fence of arms and collarbones. Girls behind the curtain, sliding the plastic cover, slim metal clinking, metal rings collapsing. Some guy had put his face close to mine. I went into the washroom to laugh it off and saw the shipwrecked girls. Maybe the guy had tried the same thing with them.

I keep my voice low but worry I'm being too quiet. I notice how loud the engine is, not just the engine but the bus floor. Beneath the floor, the tires, the road itself. Out of the sound, there are peonies growing. Massive, fully double flowers.

"I'm sorry for calling."

The light at the intersection turns dark green. Foliage of silver car casings.

"We went to the same high school." M's voice blooms from the phone. "I was a grade younger, but I saw Johnny around at parties. He was in a relationship at the time."

Blue clots appear on the line. Her words like blue blood in my stream, all my veins turn into lakes at the confluence of those words. I wasn't told this would happen. When M finishes, I thank her and hang up.

My professor once said that anyone who showed up late to his lectures would be put on the spot and expected to sing. He was joking, but sometimes, I hope otherwise. Sometimes, I imagine pulling back the narrow oak doors to forty half-shut eyes and tapping my umbrella on the linoleum, dripping, singing, tossing my umbrella to the professor and slipping my bag off my shoulder, freeing myself, spinning once, twice, shaking my damp hair loose. I want him to look at me. All of them—they will be surprised by my voice. Slapping against the ground, each step a wet tea bag. I seat myself at the end of a row of desks.

So, I'm being observed. I am under observation. Had I done something to draw attention to myself? Perhaps I have always been watched but only now become a threat. I don't know what these thoughts mean. It is Johnny they are interested in.

The two of us stand in front of an empty lecture room. Everyone, including the professor, has flitted off to recite lines of poetry or tie strings of thread on bicycle tires.

"You're wearing heels," Johnny says.

On my boots are the corpses of the morning's winged insects. "You don't think maybe you've shrunk?" I snap. "Someone called about you."

"Who?" Johnny lowers his chin to meet my gaze. "Who?"

"Someone you went to school with." I brush the grass off with my hands. I am so open, it is disgusting. I have nothing to hide, no shame.

"I'm popular among the ladies," Johnny says, grossly.

Johnny is like a child next to me. For the first time, I know him.

He scowls. "Are you in danger?"

"No. I don't think so."

Johnny walks away from campus. "Do you believe that?" he says. "I am a dangerous man?"

Once again, I'm following his lead. I notice his hair is fluffier—he got it cut; it makes him appear much younger. My knees shake chasing him down that bygone slope of adolescence. I wonder if I ever passed Johnny on the street when we were children. Maybe some spring day riding the city bus to High Park. Standing on the balls of my feet under a cherry blossom tree, blowing life into pale pink scales. A boy passing by with his mom. Would he have noticed me then?

But I would have been riding with my parents, hiding my eyes beneath the chewed brim of a hat as we stood counting quarters on the steps of the bus, the stubby ends of my hair sticking out like a porcupine's quills.

I want to reach back and hold all of him.

I have no idea how far we walked to get to Johnny's place from campus, but my shoulders are sore from carrying my textbooks in my backpack, and I can feel the muscles above my knees twitching.

"You know," Johnny begins slowly, lingering by his door. "I would have married her. I don't think we ever fought."

There is heartbreak in his voice, as when one confuses the shadows of raindrops in the pond for tadpoles. He seems almost to become a different person. My eyes fix on the beige-and-white room past his arm, the four corners of the ceiling filling me with unease.

"I thought you were a spy. I thought she sent you to find out about me."

I feel like an ant in a pit, struggling to crawl out of the sand flowing from Johnny's mouth, the hill of his back.

"Have you tried to speak to her?" I ask.

Johnny, leaning against the door frame, throws one leg casually over the other. "That girl who called you? You know she's actually crazy. I know them all from high school."

Past Johnny's arm, the room enters strangely into my vision. It means to go on forever, closer and closer, drawing us both into its yellow throat. In the depths of the room, I see my figure moving; now and then, I bend and reach below the kitchen counters, my very transparency lending a soft balance and harmony to the picture. Johnny takes my bag from my shoulders and hangs it over the back of a chair. My figure and the background are unaffected, dim and intangible, yet at this moment, my figure turns to face the door, to face me; my own face shines a bright light at the centre of my reflection.

Johnny sets his tote on the ground by the chair and removes his keys and wallet. "Well?" He stands back up again, all without moving from the door frame. "Do you want to go for a walk?"

Dim in the gathering darkness, individual shapes reach our eyes like folded ballerinas. Raccoons lugging their slow bodies beneath parked cars, plastic shovels standing upright in playground sand. We press forward into the night paradise, sinking through the city.

Now that Johnny has begun his confession, he will not stop until he is satisfied with the story. There is none of the heartbreak from his earlier speech. "You know she has a blog?"

Even in darkness, I can tell we are in a rich part of downtown. Many of the houses have floor-to-ceiling windows without curtains. The owners take satisfaction in the simple fascination of passersby. Such displays of modernity always make me feel that I am *passing by*, but my feelings are proof of the free, uncontrolled fantasy that these streets offer.

"They don't know anything about my relationship. *She left me.*"

Silver pours from the fence across the street from us—a speeding car, leaving us in silver exhaust, *she left me* gone just as fast. Dots of silver on the road. Bricks fly against the windows, transforming the street. Silver dribbling from jutting pipes. I am caught in silver refraction.

Miraculously, Johnny and I reach the bottom of a stone staircase. We step in sync to the right to let a jogger pass before beginning our ascent. "But why me?" I finally ask. "Why call me?"

"Careful." Johnny places a hand against my back. "We're being followed."

"Followed?"

"*Haunted.*"

My arms are deep in my sleeves. Even with my heeled boots on, I am almost a head shorter than Johnny. Quick, nonsense words bounce off my tongue. Johnny bends and kisses me.

Pine trees bending, needling the wind. Pine needles scattering, trees bending in the wind.

03

"THERE ARE MILLIONS of gallons of red blood cells in the human body," Johnny says. He's looking at his phone.

Resting on an amber couch, he has his coat open but his hat on. There is a student asleep next to Johnny, curled close to the radiator, knees tucked, face hidden by a wool toque with the university's logo sewn on it. A black cord snakes from the top of the student's backpack to the wall behind the couch. There are more students huddled over banquet tables. Chandeliers hang from a curved dome with carved ceiling beams. Dark oil portraits in Renaissance-style picture frames adorn the cream, panelled walls. Antique junk, unmaintained but not forgotten. Limp at our ankles, black cords trail in various directions, revealing the room's electrical impulses—I lift my heels and discover fine lines of salt, wavering white flowers.

"You had to search that up?" I ask.

"I saw a girl with her pants on backwards." Johnny takes off his hat and sees me staring. "It's getting long."

I tell him it's only been a week since he got his last haircut. He tells me the girl was wearing jeans.

"Are you staying over tonight?" he asks.

"Isn't that the plan?"

He shrugs. "Maybe you changed your mind."

Johnny sticks his hat in his coat pocket and my bag on his shoulders. I follow him out of the student lounge and down a bicycle ramp. The temperature is starting to warm. Three tourists dressed in colourful parkas step onto the ramp after us. One of the women removes the fur trim from her hood and wags the strip around like a ferret tail. The man next to her, whom I presume to be her husband, is listening intently to their guide, occasionally throwing awed glances up at the balustrade. I turn away, thinking of my parents, whose faces I want to include in this bright weather.

With his head down, looking at directions on his phone, Johnny slowly makes his way out of campus with me until we reach the university's front gates, where the campus walkway joins the city sidewalk. I remain on the cobbled walkway, not wanting to exit onto the cement path just yet. I always relish the feeling of this privilege, stalking through the withered fields of the campus, skirting around the muddy patches to get to class. Now, no one is on the street except us.

"Last time I was here," I say, "a man bumped into me and steadied himself by giving me a hug."

"That way's Yorkville, too ritzy for you." Johnny looks up suddenly.

"What?"

"Where do you want to go?" he asks.

"Why don't we make dinner?" I suggest.

"What would we make?"

"I don't know. I just think it'd be fun."

We make a detour and turn back toward Johnny's apartment. Both of us are sweating by the time we get to his place. Johnny lifts his sweater over his head and discards it on his couch. He rummages through the cabinets below the sink, white undershirt riding up his back. I lean against the doorway, ear glued to the frame, and hear clearly the sound of whistling. Thin, whistling steps, like narrow feet sprinting across flat water. I'm absorbed in identifying the source when Johnny stands holding two reusable bags—impressive for someone who doesn't have any hand towels or a garbage can for the washroom.

The way to the store is down a steep slope. Johnny doesn't think it's necessary to tell me which grocery store we're headed to. I ask him to go slower. He takes nimble steps. He lunges. "Stop," I plead. He lunges forward with his long legs, bending one knee at a time. His movements remind me of a crab, advancing at a desultory, dreamy pace, even after amputating its own claw. Perhaps there are crabs dwelling among the reeds by the ravine below the sidewalk's edge, for there are many crumpled cans to hide in until the next molting cycle. I gaze down at the shallow waterline, at the vague sand.

By the time the automatic doors of the grocery store sense us, I am already disappearing into the produce. Me and my cabbage head. Off to dig for bamboo shoots behind the hills, the orange mounds, pagodas of fruit. Leaves shimmer like jade under a fresh spray of water. Strings of water droplets surround me, so still, as if the produce has never been touched.

I pick out two slices of cake with flavours unfamiliar to me: banana dolce and mascarpone. The slices I choose are packaged behind the counter, each container given a thank-you sticker and handed to me with a simple ribbon on top. I hook my fingers through the ribbons, the containers swinging like big ornaments.

"I should've made you wait outside." Johnny proffers our basket, which now has a box of pasta, eggs, cereal, and pancake mix. I hover over the uneven placement of items with my precious gifts and decide to carry the cakes myself, should they jostle around too much and be ruined.

We join a short line at the checkout and Johnny turns the conversation to money. We can have multiple variations of the same item; we don't have to choose one or the other. He turns my attention to the orange and red candy bars on the front-end racks; I stare at our cashier's rising sleeve as she reaches to scan each item on the belt, pretending to consider his offer. The crooks of the cashier's arms are covered in eczema, and the continuous back-and-forth motion of her uniform sleeves is chafing her irritated skin. She seems more alive than either me or Johnny, I think, then I feel guilty for staring.

Johnny's excitable way of viewing money as something not fully real and at times disgustingly easy to obtain is so unlike that of my parents and even my friends that I can't join him inside his excitement. I feel a mottled layer of resin glaze over me and start to fidget with my fingers, scraping my nails beneath my cuticles. I want to be out of the store and into the day's fading brightness. We still have dinner to think about.

I start to flip through the comics like I did as a child. "My parents never let me buy these ..." But I can't get myself interested enough in the drawings.

Johnny gives his bags a shake to open them up and splits the groceries between them evenly. He plucks the cakes from me and places them on top. He takes my hand next and holds it in his, the straps of the bag digging into the skin of my other hand.

"I'm learning Italian," he says. "'Stanco' means 'tired.'"

"I am stanco," I complain.

"You should teach me to swear in Chinese."

"I don't know how."

"You've never sworn in Mandarin?"

"The only time I speak it is with my parents."

"Don't you have Asian friends?"

"Who speak English. Or Canto."

We cross the road, uphill. Forcing ourselves against wind and endless asphalt. The lights in this part of the city are different from the lights on campus; too bright, they seem to float up against the sky.

"A homeless man threatened to kill me today," Johnny says, as if explaining something to me. "He followed me to class."

"Is he following you now?"

"I'm currently being murdered."

"Too bad about Johnny. He always held my hand."

Johnny remains silent for the rest of our walk. Whenever I glance at him, he's frowning, looking away. We pass under a metal bridge, my nose picking up the ruddiness of paint and gas, fumes from graffiti still damp on the tunnel wall. We shuffle over the cooing of pigeons, finding feathers, quills, narrow tubes stabbed through crumpled plastic lids. Cars shed their bright shells below the bridge, the colours of their paint falling away into darkness some distance before they pass us. Pedestrians travel on the opposite side of the tunnel, set off in purple. My stanco feet.

Not only does Johnny invite me into his apartment this time, he also sets the bags atop his dining table and passes me his groceries one by one. I pull open the cabinet doors and slide the jars, boxes, and cans onto the shelves. There is enough space inside the cabinets that I can arrange things however I like. Johnny opens the fridge, and it's my turn to pass him the eggs, butter, two bags of milk, and the cake boxes. Johnny slides the carton of eggs toward the very back. He swivels on his heel and flips up the plastic cover on the side door for butter. He clears a shelf so the cakes can sit on a flat surface and looks for another place to put his condiments, raising tear-moistened eyes toward the dim fridge light. I imagine him all alone on a winter night. All alone at night when the sounds of the city merge with the undulating flow of water.

Johnny sweeps his gaze over the new contents of his fridge. "Want to go out for dinner instead? Actually do something fun?" He smiles at me without the slightest hint of meanness. "I got some money from the government," Johnny says. "Some tax stuff. I'm rich."

"I do my taxes," I say.

"What do you want to eat?"

"Anything. Anything is fine with me."

My affection is a modest lamp, warm in the night full of human suffering. This is my sin—easily sentimental, with no monthly electricity bill or rent to worry over.

"I'm taking you out to dinner. I have the money."

"You don't have any windows." I can't hide my disappointment.

"You don't like my place?"

"Why can't we just eat here?"

"You said you didn't like this place."

"It's cold."

"Why's your shirt so thin?"

"It's not."

"Put on a sweater."

"I don't have one."

"Take one of mine."

"In your room?"

"Check the closet."

I turn my back to Johnny and walk to the bedroom, wanting to slam the door behind me and hide under the covers, but those aren't my sheets and this isn't my home. His banjo leans against the wall, almost disappearing completely into the velvet shadows of the room. I bend and feel the strings, coarse strings, hearing the dry metallic sound they make. Sound falling off the strings like crust. A movement catches my eye, but it's just my self, redundant in a mirror, watching me. My mirror-self has gotten her fingers caught in the banjo strings. She wears a contorted smile on her face.

When I come out from the bedroom, I am repurposed in white. Johnny tells me I look good.

"This isn't too big?"

"You're a pretty girl."

He takes me for Korean barbeque somewhere with screen

dividers for a more secluded feel. I slide onto the bench and rest my elbows on the black lacquer table; Johnny takes the chair. The panels of the dividers are buried in blooming roses, forked lakes, cranes soaring over garden pines, branches of red winter plums, swaths of yellow and pink; there is no end to the screens' artistic spirit. Had my foot not bumped against the power bar by the bench, I would have missed the small tear in the corner of the screen, and the insect moving quickly over the watercolour landscape like an ox-drawn carriage, a little lord escaping across a lake, chased by flames. I am about to ask Johnny if he thinks the screen is genuine when a middle-aged waitress appears with our food. I move the cups of water on the table diligently while Johnny receives the tray.

The first piece of fish I try to cook burns right away. I scramble for the tongs, shredding the fish, scattering the white flakes. I stare, stupefied, as the parts of the fish that haven't yet charred plummet through the holes on the hot plate. Johnny uses chopsticks to pass me a piece of chicken.

The meal goes on like this, with more staff attending to us than I have ever experienced when eating alone. Shadows slide over the screen as people pass behind it. Different waitresses come to top off our water or to change the hot plate, lifting the old one out and tossing water on the fresh plate. Water explodes into steam, hissing. They bow slightly before backing out with our dirty plates.

"If I got to choose, I'd be a straight white man," I announce.

"Don't say that," Johnny says. He reminds me he comes from a poor family.

Johnny scrapes at the hot plate with the end of his chopstick. "People want to be oppressed so bad. You know what I mean? None of these people called me or my sister when she got human trafficked."

His words catch me off guard.

"I mean, she nearly got trafficked. I held her in my arms when she was beaten. No one called, none of these people who I thought were my friends. Now they're so fucking concerned about this?" He flips his chopsticks around and begins to scrape with the other end. Black crust forms around the ivory colouring of the chopsticks. "They said she was making it up."

"I'm sorry," I manage to say.

"It has nothing to do with you."

"I shouldn't have told you about the call," I say, lowering my face. Once again, my eyes flicker to the screen.

"Do you believe them?" Johnny asks. "I never hurt her. I didn't even know she was talking about me. Telling people. None of our friends asked my side of the story."

Johnny looks calm. He tells me to finish my food.

"Who called?" he asks.

04

FALL UNDER A WELL-AIMED BLOW; fall into a spell.
Johnny grazes my lip with his thumb. "You're so cold. Your
lips are purple." His voice lingers in my ears like pool water.

"Why don't you grow a beard?" I ask him.

Freshly shaven, Johnny rests his chin in the notch between
my collarbones. Each word he speaks digs into me. His words
become the sound of train wheels, whisking me away from
withered fields into purple tranquility. I lose myself, sucked
into the city like this, underground.

Afterwards, Johnny lends me a long shirt to sleep in, and
I change in his washroom. I find a hole in the shirt as I slip the
cotton over me, pointing my finger at my toes through the hem.

Moths cling to the screen of the washroom window like
eggroll flakes at the bottom of a dessert tin, smooth and feath-
ery. I rub the inside of the screen, touching the moths the way
Johnny touches me, rubbing the body between the flattened

wings. Two hours out of the city, electrical towers stick out from the earth like feathered antennae. Forewings and hind wings overlapping to create different shades, distant hills, sea glass and cognac.

Johnny lifts the hair on the side of my head with his little finger. We are seated upright in his bed. He props his elbow against a pillow and asks me if I believe in capital punishment.

I ask if he believes in ghosts.

There is blood the second time. Johnny goes to bring me water from the sink. I flatten my wings and listen; I can tell the sink is circular from the endless sound of water.

⁂

Johnny won't eat the eggs I made despite my labour of love. Smoke circles the vent-less basement. We are like illustrations drawn on carbon paper in the grey room.

Johnny makes buttermilk pancakes. He's cleaning the frying pan when I remember the grocery store cakes. He says they're basically the same as his pancakes but not as fresh. He says I can bring my cakes home with me.

"My father brought me back a knife from Iraq," Johnny says over his shoulder. He finished eating before I did and is washing his plate, which still has its price tag stuck to the bottom. I feel uncomfortable eating off Johnny's plastic plates with his bendy forks. What's the point of having a kitchen without a nice set of kitchen tools? It's not that his tastes are too lowbrow for me. Johnny's furniture, his wares, have no weight. He's set for a quick move once his lease reaches a year. But even a year together, a year, will be a long time, will satisfy me—a moth clinging to the screen, drawn by weakness to his window. When it's daylight, I'll go home.

I ask Johnny to describe the knife to me, but he says he doesn't remember how it looks. He's not trying to remember, and that makes me all the more desperate. "My sister gave me a switchblade," Johnny says, bringing me over to his desk. He picks up an olive-handled blade and rushes the blade at me, my stomach. He places his hand on my back and makes fast jabbing motions with the blade.

Poor sad-eyed Johnny under the kitchen light. Broken-down memories on the tiled floor.

Johnny's voice has become really soft, fawning even. The hand that reaches me quivers with concern. "Your food is getting cold," his voice is saying. Sitting across from me at the table, Johnny's face bears the marks of having stayed up all night. I can't stop myself from stretching my arm out and touching his face. The sound his skin makes when I touch it is like the scratching of hollow branches. He moves at once and slides open the backyard door: "Something is under the deck. Listen! Where is your mom? She told me to wait for her. The food is getting cold."

"My mom?" I ask, surprised.

"I thought you were your mom," my dad explains. "Where have you been?" He looks at me carefully. Wrinkles run down his face like silver dust. At the sight of my dad's tired face, my consciousness becomes gradually obscure; without knowing why, I keep twisting my neck around and around, trying to get a better view of the room.

"What was in the backyard?" I ask.

"You should eat now before your food gets cold."

Flattened against the backyard screen, our smoke tree looks larger, engorged with shadows, unpleasant like a pregnant spider.

"Do you remember when we lived in a basement?" I lift a pancake from my plate with chopsticks. I never knew my dad could make pancakes. I take a bite and it's really weird: it looks like a buttermilk pancake but tastes like jiānbǐng.

"Do you remember," I whisper uneasily, for I haven't decided whether it's really my dad before me or a dream, "the playground near our basement apartment. That's where you dug up the switchblade you gave me. Do you remember that switchblade?"

"No."

At that blunt answer, the front door opens and my mom comes in. She drops her coat from her shoulders onto the floor, along with her lunch bag and purse.

"The food has grown cold," my dad says in Mandarin. Fàn doū liáng le.

His nagging is annoying. "We never find anything on the ground anymore," I say.

"We didn't have a car. We had to walk everywhere, so of course we found more things on the ground," Mom says while scooping a heap of rice onto her plate. I didn't realize she had already joined us at the table. She sets her plate down and goes to draw the curtains over the sliding doors, hiding the backyard from view. "Were you going to sit in the dark all night?" The moment she turns on the light, the kitchen rises from its earlier strange trance.

Bathed in the amber glow of the overhead light, the surface of the table gives off its own lustre, ablaze with colourful dishes spread across its vast, smooth surface, all my favourites: fried egg and chives, sweet and sour spare ribs, pickled red chilies, fish in black bean sauce. Rising in my way is a roundish shape surrounded by mushroom petals; the lofty white mountain towers in front of me, and from its summit, beyond my range of sight, I can hear my mom saying between bites, "I'll never forget when you found twenty dollars." Nà me duō qián! "So much money!"

"Don't talk anymore," my dad shushes her. "Your stomach will hurt if you eat so much air."

I stare in wonder at the mountain of rice, trying to ascertain the direction of my parents' voices. "What about the switchblade?" I ask. Wind disperses my question over glistening long grains.

"I was scared someone would ask us where we got that money." My mom swallows with a gulp.

I frequently dream from the perspective of ants, where I'm lowering myself into a construction site and discovering silver coins jutting forth from the dirt and rocks. The alcoves of the cave shine with nickels, dimes, big quarters. I remove the coins like chipping mussels from a coastline boulder. I yank them quick, carting them up toward that round skylight, toward home, exposing them to air. But I always know when I'm dreaming. A rogue wave dragging me out to sea. An ocean hand scratching my back, hard enough to break my shell, waking me, turning everything black. My own hand scratching me so hard, the hurt wakes me up.

⁎⁎

I sit upright on Johnny's bed with a pillow tucked behind my back. We're watching a movie he's seen before but I haven't. The ceiling light is off, and the movie, black and white, shines its vacant silver light as though through a lampshade. It's a humid, cloudy night. Johnny peels back the seal on a box of cookies and eats quietly over his laptop, catching crumbs with his palm. I sit next to him, feeling the heat from his laptop fan on my thigh.

"What do you think about that stuff with his daughter?" Johnny asks regarding the director.

I have never seen any of Woody Allen's movies before tonight and probably won't be watching more on my own. Instead of commenting on this *stuff* that Johnny is undeniably invested in, I tell him, "I prefer watching with subtitles." Seeing that he cannot coerce my sympathy, he turns away from me and stares fixedly at the screen. Johnny continues to speak with enthusiasm between lines of dialogue. "Some of the stuff they say about his work is true." He isn't defending anyone. "It's all allegations."

Johnny pauses the movie to get something to eat. I put my socks on and join him in the kitchen. He passes me a bowl and spoon for cereal and we take our seats across from each other at the table. He scrolls on his phone the entire time we eat, then tells me not to hide behind the cereal box. "You look like you're scared of me." He scowls. I answer that it's a big box, it's family sized, but he still looks mad. "I don't care what people say," he says.

"What—about us?" I ask.

"I don't care. You can tell people whatever." Johnny wears a strangely relaxed expression. "I just don't want you to rush into anything. Think about it, do you really want people to know you're with me? I'm depressed. People actually think I'm a rapist."

I feel a stab in my heart, a wave of repulsion. How could I have suspected nothing when M called? She said, "We saw you with Johnny." Maybe none of this would be happening if we had not been seen.

"Let's finish the movie," Johnny says.

Moths cling to the screen of the washroom window above the bathtub. Below the window, traces of mildew appear like yellow chrysanthemums along the square bath tiles, water dripping from the shower head. Wondering if they're alive, I strike at the moths with my fist. The moths turn pale green and silver when I hit them, though they still do not fly away. I stand forlornly before those moths on the window screen.

05

BURNING LIGHTS LEAD UP gradually sloping rows of seats like night-blooming flowers reflecting the moonlight. It's cold in the theatre; I lay my coat gingerly over my knees and settle into my seat at the back of the auditorium. It's a deep room, full of slants. Sound rumbles from within the darkness, not unlike the echoing wheels on a train ... If I close my eyes, I can feel my seat sliding in the direction the train is moving in. Images move in strokes, strikes, against the windowpane, landscapes flitting dimly past.

When my parents were children, there was one theatre for all the screenings in their town. Since film reels were state-owned, the theatre had no library of its own. Reels circulated within the district on a loan basis, delivered by messengers on bikes; the rarity of these reels was a source of pride for anyone making the deliveries, so the messengers would often find themselves chased by children and adults alike as they cycled down the dirt paths.

My parents watched the same films over and over in the theatre courtyard on long benches in front of a white wall. Screens could also be hung on string between trees, and films were often watched this way in the summer. In the winter, they huddled close together in cotton-padded coats, enthralled by the soft light falling from the sky as their own world became gradually whiter. Each time the reel needed to be changed, the audience would jump from their seats, stomping their feet and trampling the ground in order to warm their legs, leaving behind a muddy confusion of footprints. The sounds their feet made could be heard long distances away—*deng, deng, deng*. My parents' world of forty years ago left numerous memorable landscapes on my impressionable heart. I imagine my parents sitting on opposite sides of the screen, suspended light between them—and now, myself, in the theatre, chasing after a shifting horizon.

People entering the auditorium float like dark spots in my vision, their silhouettes eclipsing small fractions of the screen each time. I hold my ticket tightly, waiting for the movie to begin.

That's when I see Johnny. I know right away that it's him. He's with someone I don't recognize—I try to avert my gaze but can't. I'm pinned down by their invisible shadow—in front of the burning screen. Johnny and his date are too busy talking to notice my face, blood-burnt in the light. He hooks his arm around his date's shoulders and lifts the hair on the side of her head with his—

To escape those memories, I decide to leave the theatre.

My legs stretch to their full length, but I sink deeper into my seat.

Johnny must be with M. What are they doing together? I haven't heard from M since that unexpected phone call. I haven't heard from Johnny in weeks.

He's ghosting me.

Johnny is making me into a ghost.

I am covered in a sheen of sweat by the time the movie ends. I stand outside the auditorium in a hypnoid state, directly above a floor light, my body revealed from the underside. I wait as the crowd pushes out from the double doors.

I want to hold Johnny in this silence, this absence. Together we'll wallow in the lack he created.

I will make him face my ghost.

Johnny exits first and passes right by me. Air slips from my mouth. The face that comes into view behind Johnny turns white. I turn white—upon seeing myself. It's my face. All the colour drains from my face. The theatre flooded, floating with leeches, the colour sucked from my face. Drops of blue, a downpour of thought, washing, draining, dissolving, walls of wind in silver slashes.

Betrayed—oh!

Betrayed!

My own self could leave me!

Every light is a reflection, a mirror. A silver screen

throwing your body at you. Your body taken from you, split into images, shown to you. White sheet hanging between two poles, your parents' backwards call, on opposite sides of the future. Out of your small mouth, you speak of the past.

As you are in your dreams: negative, polarized. The future overcomes the past.

I don't forgive her. I don't forgive my self. I know this is not the first time she has left. Reflecting me in endless numbers, stealing my memory. Lessen me, overcome me. Repeating my memory in fragments, exile me.

A room of solitude, multitude: a face I recognize as my own—she sees me.

part 02

01

SOFT RED WHEAT breaks through my dormant reflection on the windowpane. I press my cheek into the dreaming pillow; beyond, the sky is the colour of artichoke hearts. In the trees—the downy trees covering the woods with white mist—I see my cousin hiking on a grass slope overwhelmed by spreading yellow flowers. Before she can motion for me to join her, I'm already off the train and submerged in spring sunshine, inhaling memory, mycelium, fiddlehead fern half unfurled. To remember is to deny memory—to remember is to reimagine, restructure, recombine. Only through memory's silver window can my cousin reappear. The soft, round nose, the open shell of her ear, a droplet of sweat on her temple, the skin there a little shiny, a little pink, never anything but enchanting. My hand is small in hers; in the pale grass, she harvests a fistful of black hair from the field and wraps it around her wrist like a circle of leeches.

My parents kept their decision to emigrate a secret from the family until a week before our flight. I was happy not to have to complete that day's homework and immediately went to tell my cousin. When my cousin heard, she brought her little finger to my hair and began splitting the strands, building a lattice from the temple down. I couldn't see what she was doing, but my head moved with each tug. When she was done, she guided my hand down the flat braid and told me we were going for a walk. I was more than happy to accompany her—while she was older than me by only a year, my cousin was precise and clear-headed in a way I could never be. For example, she knew to dip a wooden toothpick into a vial of her mom's stinky eyebrow tint for application and to eat black sesame for shiny eyes. Every time we went for a stroll, she would take my hand solicitously, and I would tighten my grip around hers. The combined sound our slippers made was rhythmic. Whenever we stood against the wall of her building, people would come and pat our heads. "This is my sister," my cousin would say by way of introduction, tā shì wǒ mèi mei, and just like that, I belonged everywhere.

I followed my cousin, not expecting that we would be stopped by a crowd of people gathered outside the building, and I collided with her. Everyone was whispering into their palms and looking suspiciously sweaty. There was even a police car blocking off the road. The dizzying flow of voices was making me anxious, so I tugged on my cousin's hand, ready to shrink back into the building.

My cousin shifted, then plunged forward. "Don't look, or a ghost will haunt you," she yelled as we ran. A ghost? We dodged our way through the crowd and across the gravelled courtyard, stopping with our hands on our knees behind a hedge. Out of breath, my cousin repeated only one word of what she said—*guǐ*—ghost, like a white snake protruding from the bud of her mouth. Later she told me that a girl had fallen from a window and cracked her head open on the pavement. That's what those people were there to see. The girl's nǎo jiāng was on the pavement: a little shiny, a little pink.

Children from the village were fishing for frogs in the pond. I rolled up my pants to join them in the water, but as soon as I took my first step, my toes squished into something soft and jellylike, causing me to slip and fall. Soaking wet, I looked up and saw my cousin kneeling by my side. I could not see her clearly through the hair covering my eyes, but I could see her mouth, scattering—*g-u-ǐ*—and all the children were kneeling—their eyes hidden by blood and hair.

Years later, when I asked my mom about the girl who fell from my cousin's building, she stared at me full of suspicion. She hadn't heard about the accident. I recalled the record-breaking temperatures, the countryside heat embroidering flowers in my vision. My mom threw a dirty rag into the garbage can. She told me she remembered reading about a car crash that had killed a baby—maybe I got it confused with that? Her disregard upset me. I'd thought that I would finally get some answers.

I ran over to my dad, who had just come home from his job at the warehouse. He was holding his hand in a weird way. I started to ask him about the girl, but he would not listen. He went into the kitchen and started yelling. All at once, I was afraid: Was it possible that I was wrong? I locked myself in the washroom and propped my elbows on the counter. An ant was crawling on the mirror. It stopped in my iris like a second pupil. I held my finger over my eye and rolled my fingertip on the glass in a circle.

I used to take the train into the countryside every summer. Children slapped on the windows with greasy palms, holding up baskets of apples and jujube for sale. They pinched for coal on the railroad, sticking the sooty pieces into burlap bags. The yellow mountaintops, straw hats in the rice paddy, all would fall away in the long tunnel of time.

Eventually, the train would pull into a snow country. The cold voices of my teachers would pour through the window, telling me, "You're writing your name wrong. That's not your name *here*."

Here, *here*. Snow confused one place for another. Snow covered my name.

✳

I arrive home from my commute to find my sister alone at the kitchen table, staring at the backyard. The dark glass hangs her over the grass; all our furniture floats outside. My sister looks amazed to see me, her eyes swollen and soft in the dual-blue night. The rest of the house is the same. There are the paintbrushes sticking from a cup on the windowsill. The lucky knot with its long red tassel thumbtacked to the wall. My dad's forlorn guitar collecting cobwebs.

"Yuè Yuè," my sister says. "Māma fell."

Like icy shivers, those dissolving tears on my sister's face.

One day when I was six, I was surprised to see my dad waiting at the school gates for me. I bounded over to him and grabbed onto his leg. He started to ask about my day, then, as if within him there was a sudden sunburst, he lifted me up under the armpits and sat me on his shoulders. "Your mom is pregnant again," he said.

I was delirious, laughing.

"We're moving to Canada." His words were shapeless and slow.

I pressed my cheek against his and closed my eyes. "Can you have another Yuè Yuè?" I asked. "Can you have another me?"

"Yuè Yuè," my sister says in her lovely voice. "Māma hit her head. Bàba's at the hospital with her now. I don't think they're coming home tonight."

My sister was born in the winter from a fish's mouth. I lay

in my mom's arms on the hospital bed, listening to her story: "I saw a fairy bathing in the mountain river." The fairy, xiǎo xiānnü, "folded her silk dress and left it below the branches of a peach tree. She turned into a beautiful fish and dove into the water. The splash startled a monkey that was stealing peaches. The monkey was so afraid that it dropped its peaches and ran off. You should know—that mountain belonged to the gods, so it wasn't a regular peach tree!"

I looked at my sister's small, neat head, covered in fur. "Táo Táo," I blew my sister's name over her head. The xiǎo xiānnü twirled her yellow and pink sash in the starry sky.

"Let her rest," my dad said from his chair.

The nurse came into the room and my dad stood up. "Have we thought of a name for her?" the nurse asked.

"Yes," my dad said. "Emily."

Did I have a second sister? I wondered. I pressed my hand onto my mom's belly, which was still round with peaches.

Emily asks to sleep in my bed with me, we share the one pillow on my twin bed.

"Mom's going to be okay," I tell her. "She's eaten the peach of immortality."

I DID NOT once mind living in our basement apartment; in fact, I wished the apartment were smaller.

I was born in China's central coast, across the Huángpǔ River. At night I could see pink pearls rising over the blackened water, the TV tower emitting yellow, babbling radio waves from its unique pollen-producing stamen. I've ridden the slender filament, posed for photos on the anther, fallen asleep on the sepal. I've walked on thickly branched, coarse streets, shape-shifting streets with a penchant for becoming river bodied. Water ran dense in my budding heart. Ran a semicircle, evaporated.

Connected at every corner, exclusive and intimate, those humid nights in our shíkùmén apartment, sitting in the smokeless blue of our mosquito-repelling incense; grey pebbles fell from the coil as the flame travelled—tender burning lily, the night a jade embryo—I lay between my parents on a woven bamboo mat. If we moved even slightly, the slats would pinch and pull our skin, but still, it was better than developing a heat rash.

In the space-tight apartment, the only place to hang our laundry was on racks mounted outside the window. From the outside of these three-storeyed, concrete-framed apartments, laundry hung like parasols in an umbrella shop. Such were our humble circumstances. The single valuable object my parents had in their possession was a palm-sized horse sewn from pearls, gifted to them at their wedding. The horse was made with such finesse that, despite missing a few of its pearls, it was sold by my dad for a "fair payment" before our move; everything else, from my dad's LaserDisc player to my Western-style dollhouse, was given away to neighbours.

My mom never raised a word of objection, as she believed it would be impractical to bring the horse with us. But an hour before the buyer was scheduled to arrive to make the exchange, my mom would not let us wrap the horse without finding the missing pearls—"We can't sell it like this! What kind of people would we be to sell a horse with missing pearls?" She pulled out all the desk drawers and even put the pots and pans on the floor to check the kitchen cabinets. She searched with so much frenzy that I too became invested in those hidden pearls. Boarding the plane on our last day, I foolishly believed that I could return to our apartment again to search for the pearls, that the door would open for me when I came back, that I could just walk in.

⁂

My parents were born in the year of the horse, with a pulse of fire. Smouldering, quiet. With a desire to overflow, burn.

⁂

The basement we lived in belonged to a family that, like us, had emigrated from China. The family consisted of a man, his wife, their five-year-old daughter, and the man's two aged parents.

The man I knew as our landlord worked as a hairdresser at the mall. He had a raspy voice that he was insecure about and as a result always carried a bottle of water with him. I never saw him without his water bottle, sucking on the rubber straw between every few words to moisten his throat. That straw almost never deserted his lips.

He once intercepted me on the porch when I was coming home from school. He was standing there jabbing slices of lemon into his water bottle. "How about you, Yuè Yuè?" he asked. "Do you have a favourite singer?"

I was silent, fidgeting. He smiled and gave the cap on his bottle a hard twist.

"My bàba is a good singer," I said.

"Oh?" The landlord peered down at me, his eyes orange in the afternoon sun. "Since you're just a child, you wouldn't have an ear for what counts as good singing. But you should be praised—it's good—very good!—to have so much devotion to your parents!" He sucked on his lemon water. "As for my daughter, it's better that she doesn't say impulsive things." After he said this, he held the door open for me to come in.

The landlord's wife was a computer technician who worked at the same mall. The electronics repair shop she worked at not only provided service at a fraction of the regular cost but also sold pirated CDs in flimsy plastic sleeves. Once a month the woman would bring home a plastic baggie of movies for her daughter to watch, and her daughter, a rather clingy girl, would invite me to watch them with her. She would tell me to wait for her at the foot of their staircase while she ran to grab the movie she wanted. Waiting with nothing to do, I'd find the woman leaning demurely against the sliding doors, smoking a cigarette. I'd follow the woody smell into their living room, inching my way past the coffee table, the couch, the glass cabinet full of plates. If the woman saw me at those times, she never said anything.

Watching those pirated movies always made me feel strange. I had no idea the movies were illegally recorded at the cinema, and the ghosts I thought were in the movies were in actuality the silhouettes of unsuspecting audience members.

I was never allowed to go upstairs with the girl. Whether we were watching a movie together or drawing with crayons, it would have to be in their living room or our basement. The girl's grandparents especially did not like seeing me in their house, using their furniture. Once, the old woman even said, "It's only because we're from China too that we'd be so kind as to let people like you live in our house."

I didn't know what she meant by that. Because my mom had been a doctor when we were in China, the landlord's family was always coming down to ask her opinion on things. They'd wake us up in the middle of the night because their daughter had caught a cold and wet the bed. I'd press my pillow over my ears and still hear the circular beating of hearts in our basement, still hear the old woman saying "people like you," in Mandarin, nǐ men zhè zhǒng rén.

Dandelions grew in the plume grass; the hills shone yellow. We woke to a snowstorm of seeds whenever spiders dreamt of silk.

Pitch-dark, without any moonlight, the old woman's face rushes forward in my memory. The pale view of her high cheekbones is beautiful, and her slanted nose, and those upward-tilting lashes. But isn't it a young face? Whose face am I remembering?

I remember one incident: a lost earring. The landlord's entire family spent the day searching. I could hear their raised voices through the floor. They were shuffling the furniture and stomping up and down the stairs. A full hour passed before things finally quieted down and there came a rapping on our basement door. I opened the door and came face to face with the landlord's daughter. Her eyes were large and white. Floating above her was her grandma's face, large and white. "Little girl, little girl. Did you take it?"

Nothing terrified me more than that voice. "No," I said.

"Don't just say no," the old woman scolded me. "You only know how to say one word of English. Are you stupid?"

"I didn't steal it," I said in Mandarin. "It wasn't me"— bú shì wǒ

—sound hatched on my tongue. I imagined syllables that grew six centimetres in length; fast swimmers, they needed oxygen to survive. Chemical cues allowed them to recognize each other. A silver species of language, a shoal of words, a repetitive pattern used to prolong, respond to, substitute for, preserve. Bú shì wǒ.

Shì is a perfect syllable. Singular, whistle-quick, *shì*: used before nouns to identify, describe, amplify; used after nouns to denote place or position, to express existence. *Shì*: response; yes; correct. *Shi-shi-shi*, my mom pursed her lips. *Shi*—it's so hot even the cicadas are suffering. *Shi-shi, shi-shi*. Two weeks after the plum rain season ends, black cicada pupae emerge into adults; they can be found in the flower beds and in the trees, in the treetops, in willow trees and privet shrubs; almost transparent, breaking through murky shells.

Shī: wet.

Black cicadas completing eclosion—see how the cicada stretches its thin crystal-wings!

Long-horned grasshoppers in rattan-woven cages; bright-green crickets on *shī* leaves.

⁂

After my sister was born, we moved into one of three buildings under the same property management in a small community half an hour away by car. We also bought our first car, a Ford Taurus, for five thousand dollars.

The property had an unspoken hierarchy: there were the three-bedroom flats, the two-winged building with its two- and three-bedroom units, and finally, the bachelor building, which was where we lived. We drew much unwanted attention as the only family of four living in a bachelor apartment—we took up too much space. If someone happened to walk into the lobby when we were waiting for the elevator, my dad would take the stairs. "How about we see who can get there faster?" he would challenge me with a jaunty smile before turning down the hall, his back to me, growing smaller and smaller.

I glanced doubtfully between the stairway and the elevator. The carpet had a pervasive smell of medicine that made my eyes water. The smell would permeate my vision; for a few moments half my visual field would be blocked before being replaced by a headache. In anguish, I pressed the elevator button again and again. Next to me, I could hear the sloshing of the milk in the bottle, then the bottle being hit against the stroller. Emily was already six months old. My hand trembled as I pressed the button. I was convinced that by the time we got upstairs, my dad would be unrecognizable.

Light reflected brilliantly against the white walls of our living room. My parents slept in the den while Emily and I took the bedroom. I spent most of my time looking out the window; I'd step onto the heater to climb onto the window-sill, then slide the glass open just wide enough to catch the breeze. I dangled my feet over the floor, feeling the sun on my back. Our car looked like a dark-green beetle in the parking lot. I couldn't see them, but vertical cracks were appearing in the trunks of all the trees. When the leaves thinned and turned pale yellow, I mistook want for hope.

Want: specific to absence and lack. Hope: expectation; belief that something is obtainable.

Want: Sitting on a mud wall in the countryside, I kicked my sandals off and watched them fall—*poof-poof*—onto the rust-orange dirt. Grasshoppers leapt like waterworks under the high sun; there were so many grasshoppers that the long weeds growing from the cracks in the pavement swayed, and pools of water rippled. So many that there was no way to bike without catching the grasshoppers beneath my tires.

My cousin swatted the air in annoyance. "Look at them," my cousin said into the palm of her hand. "Their eyes look softly attached. What do you think they see?" Her hand was oozing with fluid. Oddly, the grasshoppers' legs fell off when we fed them live worms.

We played outside until the dirt turned blue, stirred up like mist by summer insects. Jiā Jiā and Yuè Yuè—there wasn't a fence we couldn't flip over; not a single gate could keep us out. When we got hungry, we'd take out a few crinkled bills and buy a bowl of liángpí to share, squat on the curb, and start slurping the cold, extremely spicy, translucent noodles. Jiā Jiā cried while she ate, stamped her feet, and pinched her own leg. She'd exhale noisily through her mouth—*haa haa*—and keep eating. When we were done, she would buy us a fried fish skewer each for the way home. I loved the fish skewers the most. The tail was flat like a chip, brittle and crunchy, always followed by a gulp of warm Sprite from a colourful plastic cup. When we needed to pee, we'd find an empty lot and pull up our skirts.

Hope: possibility, prospect, the vibratory prayer. Pine trees grew everywhere. Green needles blocked out the sky.

⁂

Dream: trees keep their memory in rings, complete, inside them.

03

THE MORNING IS wonderfully fresh from a night of rain. Between the houses, the strong smell of pine; here and there, a palpitating petal on the lawn. I decide to take a stroll through the neighbourhood before Emily wakes. The skin on her cheek where she slept against her arm is red. When I lift the blanket, she turns instinctively toward the wall with a wry smile.

I have already spoken to my dad over the phone. Emily's face was like a star next to me, half-water, half-honey, her breath so faint I couldn't bear to wake her up.

Emily and I used to share a bunk bed in our apartment bedroom. At night we'd swing our legs in an arc and knock our heels against the wall—*deng, deng*—rhythmically and in code—*deng, deng*. We shared countless untranslatable dreams back and forth: *deng, deng, deng. Deng deng deng*, until the echo faded with sleep; failed to return.

Deng-deng-deng.

Deng-deng-deng.

Wolves at the door. Wolves dressed as the person who loves you. Emily lay sideways on the pillow, her head by Mom's neck. I lay on my back, my feet pressed up against the wall.

"Māma, will you tell it different this time? I want the wolf to win."

Emily agreed with me. "Wolves are cute!"

"Children's toes are delicious when pickled!" Mom said and lunged at us.

We squealed and squealed.

We kicked our heels against the wall and laughed.

Deng—

Deng—

Deng—the door.

When the sound of knocking came from the door, I cowered like a rabbit by the shoe rack.

Deng—

Jehovah's Witnesses visited the apartment building every second Sunday. *Deng.* "Where's Mommy?" Shrivelled fingers slipped through a crack in the door to hand me a glossy pamphlet. "Are you home alone?" *Deng deng.* Urgent hands tugged on the hanging chain lock.

My mom had once mistakenly opened the door for the Witnesses, thinking our neighbours had come to tell us we'd left our keys hanging from the lock—since having my sister, she'd become more and more forgetful. Without moving a muscle in her face, the old woman at the door introduced herself and stepped into our apartment. Her hair was damp and frizzy like she had encountered a cloud on her way up. She passed her cane to her partner, and they sat down at our kitchen table. Out of instinct, my mom began to fill the kettle with water for tea and gave me a dishcloth to wipe down the table.

I could see the corner of a poster quivering, and antennas poked out. The apartment had a roach infestation. Flecks of shells on the walls, small black-brown cavities, a multiplicity of legs, antennas ... I expected my mom to remove the slipper from her foot as I'd seen her do countless times, but instead, she joined the frail women at the table with a bashful smile. From a small black purse, one of the women pulled out a leather-bound notebook and placed it in the centre of our table. Looking at it from the side, I could see the pages of the book glistened like gold.

When the old women came, they always brought books with them. I looked forward to reading the fantastical adventures described in those books. One story I read left me feeling confused, and I wanted to ask the women about it when I saw them, but when they came, they were very angry.

"She's a child," my mom tried her best to explain, the tea in her hands forgotten.

The old, white-haired woman pointed at me, finger wriggling like a mealworm.

Hoping to be helpful, I reached for the book in the old

woman's hands, but she jerked back with surprising force, and in the tussle, I accidentally scratched her with my nail. She let out a wail, a hiss, like a tire being punctured. The sound made my whole body twist. Meanwhile, my mom was spreading her palms and flapping her hands like a flying dove.

The old women in our living room wore bulletproof vests over navy uniforms. They hooked thick thumbs into the armpits of their vests and roared with laughter. Their laughter rammed into the door: DENG, DENG, DENG. Even if our apartment was dirty, it was still our home, I thought. They should take their boots off at the door. Even if they are the police, they should take off their boots. DENG, DENG, DENG. Police stomped merrily around our home. They used our windows to spy on our neighbour, went out onto our balcony, and scared off the squirrels and pigeons. DENG, DENG, DENG. Our neighbour's door came crashing down.

Our neighbour was arrested for growing weed in inflatable kiddie pools.

"It's not their fault they don't have a garden," I said.

"Life isn't fair," my dad said simply.

Deng—

The door—

Boxing Day was the first big holiday my family was able to celebrate since arriving in Canada. My dad had his eye on a plasma TV. He measured the dimensions of our living room from the kitchen table to the balcony. He relocated his desktop to face the other wall and carried all our folding chairs into the bedroom. He carried them all out like a ritual. By the time we arrived at the mall, nearly everything was sold out, the shelves emptied and shopping baskets flipped upside down. Luckily, there was still one left in stock of the TV my dad wanted. The salesperson helping us told us to stay where we were, but when he came back, he started chatting with another customer. I was hungry and tired. My headache was back. "Don't you want to watch cartoons?" My dad sensed that I was reaching the last of my energy. "You can improve your English by watching TV," he told me. I imagined my dad would watch the cartoons with me; I nodded eagerly and straightened up.

The other customer also wanted the TV my dad wanted, and the salesperson was going to sell it to him even though we had gotten there first. It was noisy with all the TV displays and video games and music. To make matters worse, Emily had started to cry; her shrill cries bounced off the walls and rattled the empty shelves. Mom was cradling and rocking Emily in one arm all while she practised her English. "No," my mom said. "No," she said firmly—but the salesperson was still going to sell the TV to the other customer. Then—like a silver coin flipping in the air—the customer called my dad a chink. *Chink*. That deep red mouth looked like a wishing well.

Wood chips dusted the carpet. Splinters jutted from the door frame. We came home from the mall to find that our apartment had been broken into. Unlike the time our neighbours were busted, only one police officer stood in our living room. Our drawers were pulled out and our clothes were strewn about the floor. I was suddenly embarrassed at not having separate sections for my underwear and my socks. The newsprint we pasted over the tiles above our stove was soaked with oil. "You can tell this family cooks Chinese," my parents often joked. The officer flipped his notepad to a fresh page and printed a few neat letters. "Did you lose anything of value?" He spoke to us as if we were in trouble. I wanted to run into our living room and cover our Christmas tree with my body. I had made the tree by cutting three sheets of cardboard into triangles, colouring them in, and arranging them on the wall. I made the ornaments by cutting patterns from ads.

—the door makes the same sound when broken down by a foot or a chisel or the weather; the wood splinters or cracks or it dampens or it sloughs over the years. My sister's heel makes the same sound as my heel when she kicks the wall or the ground when she's running or she's kicking on the door aggressively, wanting to be let in, to return to, let me in, let me back, I belong here, here is where I came from, so let me in, let me in, as anger is born from desperation, and violence sweeps all in its sorrow. Or so I dreamt.

⁂

dēng déng děng dèng dēng déng děng dèng dēng déng děng

dèng dēng déng dèng děng dēng déng děng dèng dēng déng

děng dèng dēng déng děng dèng dēng déng děng dèng dēng

déng děng dèng dēng déng děng dèng dēng déng děng dèng

dēng déng děng dèng dēng déng děng dèng dēng déng děng

dèng dēng déng děng dèng dēng déng děng dèng dēng déng

děng dèng dēng déng děng dèng dēng déng děng dèng dēng

déng děng dèng dēng déng děng dèng dēng déng děng dèng

dēng déng děng dèng dēng déng děng dèng dēng déng děng

dèng dēng déng děng dèng dēng déng děng dèng dēng déng

děng dèng dēng déng děng dèng dēng déng děng dèng dēng

déng děng dèng dēng déng děng dèng dēng déng děng dèng

dēng déng děng dèng dēng déng děng dèng dēng déng děng

dèng dēng déng děng dèng dēng déng děng dèng dēng déng

děng dèng dēng déng děng dèng dēng déng děng dèng dēng

déng děng dèng dēng déng děng dèng dēng déng děng dèng

dēng déng děng dèng dēng déng děng dèng dēng déng děng

dèng dēng déng děng dèng dēng déng děng dèng dēng déng

děng dèng dēng déng děng dèng dēng déng děng dèng dēng

déng děng dèng dēng déng děng dèng dēng déng děng dèng

dēng déng děng dèng dēng déng děng dèng dēng déng děng

dèng dēng déng děng dèng dēng déng děng dèng dēng déng

děng dèng dēng déng děng dèng dēng déng děng dèng dēng

déng děng dèng dēng déng děng dèng dēng déng děng dèng

dēng déng děng dèng dēng déng děng dèng dēng déng děng

dèng dēng déng děng dèng dēng déng děng dèng dēng déng

děng dèng dēng déng děng dèng dēng déng děng dèng dēng

déng děng dèng dēng déng děng dèng dēng déng děng dèng

dēng déng děng dèng dēng déng děng dèng dēng déng děng

dèng dēng déng děng dèng dēng déng děng dèng dēng déng

děng dèng dēng déng děng dèng dēng déng děng dèng dēng

déng děng dèng dēng déng děng dèng dēng déng děng dèng

dēng déng děng dèng dēng déng děng dèng dēng déng děng

dèng dēng déng děng dèng dēng déng děng dèng dēng déng

děng dèng dēng déng děng dèng dēng déng děng dèng dēng

déng děng dèng dēng déng děng dèng dēng déng děng dèng

dēng déng děng dèng dēng déng děng dèng dēng déng děng

dèng dēng déng děng dèng dēng déng děng dèng dēng déng

děng dèng dēng déng děng dèng dēng déng děng dèng dēng

déng děng dèng dēng déng děng dèng dēng déng děng dèng

dēng déng děng dèng dēng déng děng dèng dēng déng děng

dèng dēng déng děng dèng dēng déng děng dèng dēng déng

děng dèng dēng déng děng dèng dēng déng děng dèng dēng

déng děng dèng dēng déng děng dèng dēng déng děng dèng

dēng déng děng dèng dēng déng děng dèng dēng déng děng

dèng dēng déng děng dèng dēng déng děng dèng dēng déng

děng dèng dēng déng děng dèng dēng déng děng dèng dēng

déng děng dèng dēng déng děng dèng dēng déng děng dèng

dēng déng děng dèng dēng déng děng dèng dēng déng děng

dèng dēng déng děng dèng dēng déng děng dèng dēng déng

děng dèng dēng déng děng dèng dēng déng děng dèng dēng

déng děng dèng dēng déng děng dèng dēng déng děng dèng

dēng déng děng dèng dēng déng děng dèng dēng déng děng

dèng dēng déng děng dèng dēng déng děng dèng dēng déng

děng dèng dēng déng děng dèng dēng déng děng dèng dēng

déng děng dèng dēng déng děng dèng dēng déng děng dèng

dēng déng děng dèng dēng déng děng dèng dēng déng děng

dèng dēng déng děng dèng dēng déng děng dèng dēng déng

děng dèng dēng déng děng dèng dēng déng děng dèng dēng

déng děng dèng dēng déng děng dèng dēng déng děng dèng

dēng déng děng dèng dēng déng děng dèng dēng déng děng

dèng dēng déng děng dèng dēng déng děng dèng dēng déng

děng dèng dēng déng děng dèng dēng déng děng dèng dēng

déng děng dèng dēng déng děng dèng dēng déng děng dèng

dēng déng děng dèng dēng déng děng dèng dēng déng děng

dèng dēng déng děng dèng dēng déng děng dèng dēng déng

děng dèng dēng déng děng dèng dēng déng děng dèng dēng

déng děng dèng dēng déng děng dèng dēng déng děng dèng

dēng déng děng dèng dēng déng děng dèng dēng déng děng

dèng dēng déng děng dèng dēng déng děng dèng dēng déng

děng dèng dēng déng děng dèng dēng déng děng dèng dēng

déng děng dèng dēng déng děng dèng dēng déng děng dèng

dēng déng děng dèng dēng déng děng dèng dēng déng děng

dèng dēng déng děng dèng dēng déng děng dèng dēng déng

děng dèng dēng déng děng dèng dēng déng děng dèng dēng

déng děng dèng dēng déng děng dèng dēng déng děng dèng

dēng déng děng dèng dēng déng děng dèng dēng déng děng

dèng dēng déng děng dèng dēng déng děng dèng dēng déng

děng dèng dēng déng děng dèng dēng déng děng dèng dēng

déng děng dèng dēng déng děng dèng dēng déng děng dèng

dēng déng děng dèng dēng déng děng dèng dēng déng děng

dèng dēng déng děng dèng dēng déng děng dèng dēng déng

děng dèng dēng déng děng dèng dēng déng děng dèng dēng

déng děng dèng dēng déng děng dèng dēng déng děng dèng

dēng déng děng dèng dēng déng děng dèng dēng déng děng

dèng dēng déng děng dèng dēng déng děng dèng dēng déng

děng dèng dēng déng děng dèng dēng déng děng dèng dēng

déng děng dèng dēng déng děng dèng dēng déng děng dèng

dēng déng děng dèng dēng déng děng dèng dēng déng děng

dèng dēng déng děng dèng dēng déng děng dèng dēng déng

děng dèng dēng déng děng dèng dēng déng děng dèng dēng

déng děng dèng dēng déng děng dèng dēng déng děng dèng

dēng déng děng dèng dēng déng děng dèng dēng déng děng

dèng dēng déng děng dèng dēng déng děng dèng dēng déng

děng dèng dēng déng děng dèng dēng déng děng dèng dēng

déng děng dèng dēng déng děng dèng dēng déng děng dèng

dēng déng děng dèng dēng déng děng dèng dēng déng děng

dèng dēng déng děng dèng dēng déng děng dèng dēng déng

děng dèng dēng déng děng dèng dēng déng děng dèng dēng

déng děng dèng dēng déng děng dèng dēng déng děng dèng

dēng déng děng dèng dēng déng děng dèng dēng déng děng

dèng dēng déng děng dèng dēng déng děng dèng dēng déng

děng dèng dēng déng děng dèng dēng déng děng dèng dēng

déng děng dèng dēng déng děng dèng dēng déng děng dèng

dēng déng děng dèng dēng déng děng dèng dēng déng děng

dèng dēng déng děng dèng dēng déng děng dèng dēng déng

děng dèng dēng déng děng dèng dēng déng děng dèng dēng

déng děng dèng dēng déng děng dèng dēng déng děng dèng

dēng déng děng dèng dēng déng děng dèng dēng déng děng

dèng dēng déng děng dèng dēng déng děng dèng dēng déng

děng dèng dēng déng děng dèng dēng déng děng dèng dēng

déng děng dèng dēng déng děng dèng dēng déng děng dèng

dēng déng děng dèng dēng déng děng dèng dēng déng děng

dèng dēng déng děng dèng dēng déng děng dèng dēng déng

děng dèng dēng déng děng dèng dēng déng děng dèng dēng

déng děng dèng dēng déng děng dèng dēng déng děng dèng

dēng déng děng dèng dēng déng děng dèng dēng déng děng

dèng dēng déng děng dèng dēng déng děng dèng dēng déng

děng dèng dēng déng děng dèng dēng déng děng dèng dēng

déng děng dèng dēng déng děng dèng dēng déng děng dèng

dēng déng děng dèng dēng déng děng dèng dēng déng děng

dèng dēng déng děng dèng dēng déng děng dèng dēng déng

děng dèng dēng déng děng dèng dēng déng děng dèng dēng

déng děng dèng dēng déng děng dèng dēng déng děng dèng

dēng déng děng dèng dēng déng děng dèng dēng déng děng

dèng dēng déng děng dèng dēng déng děng dèng dēng déng

děng dèng dēng déng děng dèng dēng déng děng dèng dēng

déng děng dèng dēng déng děng dèng dēng déng děng dèng

dēng déng děng dèng dēng déng děng dèng dēng déng děng

dèng dēng déng děng dèng dēng déng děng dèng dēng déng

děng dèng dēng déng děng dèng dēng déng děng dèng dēng

déng děng dèng dēng déng děng dèng dēng déng děng dèng

dēng déng děng dèng dēng déng děng dèng dēng déng děng

dèng dēng déng děng dèng dēng déng děng dèng dēng déng

děng dèng dēng déng děng dèng dēng déng děng dèng dēng

déng děng dèng dēng déng děng dèng dēng déng děng dèng

dēng déng děng dèng dēng déng děng dèng dēng déng děng

dèng dēng déng děng dèng dēng déng děng dèng dēng déng

děng dèng dēng déng děng dèng dēng déng děng dèng dēng

déng děng dèng dēng déng děng dèng dēng déng děng dèng

dēng déng děng dèng dēng déng děng dèng dēng déng děng

dèng dēng déng děng dèng dēng déng děng dèng dēng déng

děng dèng dēng déng děng dèng dēng déng děng dèng dēng

déng děng dèng dēng déng děng dèng dēng déng děng dèng

dēng déng děng dèng dēng déng děng dèng dēng déng děng

dèng dēng déng děng dèng dēng déng děng dèng dēng déng

děng dèng dēng déng děng dèng dēng déng děng dèng dēng

déng děng dèng dēng déng děng dèng dēng déng děng dèng

dēng déng děng dèng dēng déng děng dèng dēng déng děng

dèng dēng déng děng dèng dēng déng děng dèng dēng déng

děng dèng dēng déng děng dèng dēng déng děng dèng dēng

déng děng dèng dēng déng děng dèng dēng déng děng dèng

dēng déng děng dèng dēng déng děng dèng dēng déng děng

dèng dēng déng děng dèng dēng déng děng dèng dēng déng

děng dèng dēng déng děng dèng dēng déng děng dèng dēng

déng děng dèng dēng déng děng dèng dēng déng děng dèng

dēng déng děng dèng dēng déng děng dèng dēng déng děng

dèng dēng déng děng dèng dēng déng děng dèng dēng déng

děng dèng dēng déng děng dèng dēng déng děng dèng dēng

déng děng dèng dēng déng děng dèng dēng déng děng dèng

dēng déng děng dèng dēng déng děng dèng dēng déng děng

dèng dēng déng děng dèng dēng déng děng dèng dēng déng

děng dèng dēng déng děng dèng dēng déng děng dèng dēng

déng děng dèng dēng déng děng dèng dēng déng děng dèng

dēng déng děng dèng dēng déng děng dèng dēng déng děng

dèng dēng déng děng dèng dēng déng děng dèng dēng déng

děng dèng dēng déng děng dèng dēng déng děng dèng dēng

déng děng dèng dēng déng děng dèng dēng déng děng dèng

dēng déng děng dèng dēng déng děng dèng dēng déng děng

dèng dēng déng děng dèng dēng déng děng dèng dēng déng

děng dèng dēng déng děng dèng dēng déng děng dèng dēng

déng děng dèng dēng déng děng dèng dēng déng děng dèng

dēng déng děng dèng dēng déng děng dèng dēng déng děng

dèng dēng déng děng dèng dēng déng děng dèng dēng déng

děng dèng dēng déng děng dèng dēng déng děng dèng dēng

déng děng dèng dēng déng děng dèng dēng déng děng dèng

dēng déng děng dèng dēng déng děng dèng dēng déng děng

dèng dēng déng děng dèng dēng déng děng dèng dēng déng

děng dèng dēng déng děng dèng dēng déng děng dèng dēng

déng děng dèng dēng déng děng dèng dēng déng děng dèng

dēng déng děng dèng dēng déng děng dèng dēng déng děng

dèng dēng déng děng dèng dēng déng děng dèng dēng déng

děng dèng dēng déng děng dèng dēng déng děng dèng dēng

déng děng dèng dēng déng děng dèng dēng déng děng dèng

deng

deng

deng

deng

deng

deng

deng

deng

deng

deng

deng

deng

等 PY děng

*class, grade, rank, kind, sort, wait, await, equal, equivalent,
when, till, and so on, and so forth, indicating the end, to wait
for, to await, once*

灯 PY dēng

lamp, lantern, light, valve, tube, burner

登 PY dēng

*ascend, mount, scale, publish, record, enter, her name ap-
peared on the summit, abundant harvest of syllables, take to
the threshing ground*

瞪 PY dèng

open your eyes wide, stare, glare, open

蹬 PY dēng

press down with the foot, step on, tread on, put on, pedal

噔 PY dēng

thump! thud! deng! deng!

磴 PY dèng

cliff-ledge, stone step

镫 PY dèng
stirrup

澄 PY dèng
settle, liquid settling, becoming clear, pure water

嶝 PY dèng
mountain path, hillside, path leading up

⁂

I walk on a grassy knoll, over a small hill, I take the meander-
ing path, my vision clears, like liquid settling, I follow the
water, in the creek, I stirrup the moths, I tread through the
fern, I take the stone step, I thump, I thump, I press with my
feet, I tread on the soft grass, thud, thud, I pedal forward, her
face appears, a bright syllable, a bright beckoning, indicating the end, indicating wait, her face equal to mine, her wait
equals mine, I open my eyes, I stare, I press down, I glare, I
open, I walk, on a deng, I walk over a deng, I take the mean-
dering deng, my vision deng, like deng, I follow the deng, in
the creek, I deng the moths, I deng through the fern, I take
the deng, I deng, I deng, I deng, deng on the soft grass, deng,
deng, deng forward, her face deng, a bright syllable, a bright
beckoning, deng, indicating deng, her face deng mine, her
wait deng mine, I deng my eyes, I deng, I deng, I deng, I deng.

77

I walk through the neighbourhood to the pond by the side of the road. Coniferous trees crown the water's edge. The forest floor is damp and covered in pine needles and leaf litter; there are many small mounds and pits, and broadleaf flowers are mixed in with the bracken. The water in the pond is murky and dark green; fish glide in the shadows; schools of minnows swim close to the silt near the shoreline. Mayflies, damselflies; turtles with spear-shaped heads; algae clinging like lace fingers to dead trees.

A little girl is squatting on a rock in her smoky red sweater with the sleeves rolled up. Only one side of her hair is tied in a pigtail; the other half hangs over her face. She's drilling into the mud so hard with a stick that she doesn't hear my footsteps. I don't see or hear anyone else nearby, just a swarm of midges. The weeds by the girl look trampled; I notice bits of grass stuck in her hair.

I'm about to leave when the girl turns, and from behind a curtain of black hair, her profile is revealed to me. I know her face. How? This girl can't be more than six years old. And her hair—

After my mom had Emily, she stopped doing my hair for me in the mornings before school. I managed to convince my dad to do my hair on one occasion. He used an oval brush to sweep one part of my hair up and secured it with an elastic, then moved on to the other half. I was unhappy with the uneven parting; there was a big difference in the volume of hair on each side. My dad slipped the comb into his pocket, and I heard the sound of his chair being pushed back. I went to school with my hair half up, half down. Despite the stares I was getting, I refused to remove the elastic on the one side of my head. And I didn't want to tie the other half by myself either. I was always thinking if only mom could do this ... if only Jiā Jiā were here ... if only Jiā Jiā were here! She has never seen a squirrel in her life—there are no squirrels where she lives. Isn't it hilarious that there was a time in my life when I didn't know what squirrels were?

It's my hair.

My hair catches in the branches as I run, leaving a trail of shiny, silver-black strands on the leaves. Pebbles spring up with every step, gray needles and egg-shaped cones flinging left and right. I run, leap, dash, sprint, hurtle, scamper over knots, shallow roots, stones, broken beer bottles, wild daffo-dils. I run, until I can hear the sound of cars on the road, until I reach my street. She wants me to stay with her. She wants to lure me into the woods. Into her multiplicity, her mirrors; she wants to fracture my memory and enshrine me.

Our car is in the driveway, which means Dad is home— he's probably told Emily by now—a swarm of midges, a cluster of promises. Cancer. *If* it's cancer. In the worst case, mom will have four months, maybe a year.

Ah, whose face did I see in the woods? Whose face am I forgetting?

04

FOR THE LAST HOUR, my dad has been pacing in the living room. His clothes smell like the hospital, a faint flow of antiseptic. He seems barely conscious. Emily urges him several times to sit down, to which he says, "I've been sitting all night." Wǎn shàng. Wǎn le. The sound of the caron on the *a* scooping a wedge of air from us is like a prayer bowl: wán le, the bowl tips, spills; all the tension in my dad's shoulders dissipates as he slumps onto a chair. He barely acknowledges his own voice leaving him. "I've been looking into it—I've been looking into it," he says while adjusting the buttons on his sleeves, wrists as thin as a child's.

Emily edges forward on her chair and presses her palms onto her knees. She turns her chin toward the backyard when she speaks. "We shouldn't assume the worst."

"When I was with her, she was groaning all night."

"Her face is always red. She's so healthy, there's nothing to worry about."

Listening to them, I feel my own condition worsen until I'm unable to bear the sight of the two of them. Neither my dad nor Emily notices when I leave. I head for my parents' bedroom upstairs and find the room in disarray: clothes on the bed and floor, towels drying on the curtain rod, wastebasket toppled on its side. My parents' apartment in China suffered the same thing—efflorescence on the walls, open cigarette packs stacked on the windowsill (that was back when they smoked). Whenever I try to help my parents clean, they scold me for misplacing things. Their faces scrunch up, and they say, "When you have your own house, you can decorate it however you please. Then you can invite us over and teach us all about elegance."

I shuffle the papers on my dad's desk and tuck them into the pages of his calendar. I wipe a spot of dust from his keyboard, then I turn on his computer.

In his free time, my dad brings up old family albums from the basement to scan and retouch the photos on his computer. He uses his memory as a guide for preservation: "*This* is how the sky looked. The flowers *were* this yellow. Your mom's face was *even* redder." Photos fade over time because the ink used to print them contains a light-absorbing body; even hidden away in the basement, the light reaches, washes.

Floweret, freckle, fawn. I begin with the film shot in the

nineties. On the computer, the faces of my parents' cohort remain smooth and youthful. Grinning prettily on the beach, his long hair clipped back, wearing nothing but a pair of bright-red swimming briefs, the young man next to my mom I almost mistake for my dad, then remember, he died in the water.

The high sea of memory—when my mom gazes over its blue surface, does the wave come a second time? Does death happen a second time through memory? When she speaks of her friend, my mom grins, as if standing on the beach still, her long hair clipped back. Reproduced in her—a pretty smile, the colour red. Her focus drifts—she leaves a towel on the sand, she forgets the food in the car. Does she know I'm afraid of water? I carry her longing in me as a way to carry her. The same longing courses through my dad: he raises his arms toward the leafy canopy, standing in a shaft of light. But he won't take photos of himself. He won't try to remember the camouflage bark on the London plane trees or the lily pads next to the boardwalk. When I point to the fan palms, when I scoop for minnows—I'm begging him to look. When I'm six years old and he tells me to pose for a photo by the school gates on my first day of class and I won't stand still—I'm begging him, look. Because he's looking at me, but I'm looking at him.

I'm looking at my mom through a mosquito net as she sucks on a cold triangle of watermelon. My mom eating seven lamb kebabs at once, spreading the metal skewers like a skeletal fan, pulling at the fatty, chili-dusted meat with her teeth. My mom on a steep hiking trail in a dress she sewed herself, twisted, wobbly pines behind her, imperial garden lions, horsetail waterfalls. My mom and her friends raising their proud little fists to the sky, wearing crowns of leaves on their heads.

My dad looks like a young historian as he leans against the Great Wall, binoculars slung across his shoulder, the straight bar of his glasses underlining his careful brow.

My parents' first photo together—they look like babies! Each photo is a gem. Here's another of my mom: taken on her first day of med school—her first white lab coat! The lab coat that my mom brought from China and uses only when she's giving Dad haircuts in the living room. Dad will sit on a dining chair in the middle of the room while Mom paces around him in her lab coat, taking small steps to avoid the hair on the floor. I'm not sure why she insists on wearing the coat when it's never her who gets covered in hair. When she's finished, she'll order Dad to stand so she can pat him down, then it's Dad's turn to cut her hair.

All my haircuts were given to me in the same way and so were Emily's. As a result, we had the same hairstyle growing up. Straight black hair chopped to our collarbones, craggy bangs. Until we both grew humiliated enough to learn how to cut and style our own hair.

A similar scene played out in my uncle's apartment in China: Grandpa shirtless in the middle of the living room while Grandma shaved his head, plastic sheets spread below his chair. Grandma, however, always went with my aunt for the latest perms, in a linoleum-floored salon, amid the fragrance of rosewater sprays, imitation pearl dancing in the flattering light.

Both my grandparents on my mom's side are illiterate. My grandparents are orphans who survived the great famine from 1959 to 1961. It was one of the deadliest famines in China's history, leaving millions of people dead and children without families. When I was younger, I had a habit of hitting the rims of steel bowls with my chopsticks, as if I were playing the drums. The sound would make my mom furious. "Stop that now!" she'd say aggressively. "What a terrible sound!" Then she'd tell me how Grandma was the youngest of eight children, born to an accountant who was arrested at the end of the civil war. "He worked for the Guómíndǎng," she explained. "It was a good thing they took your grandma's dad away! His wife loved him more than her own children. Every bit of food they had she would feed to him. And he had stomach issues, so he always threw it up!" Grandma, according to my mom's telling of the past, fended for herself by going door to door knocking on a metal bowl, begging for food. "Only an empty bowl can make such a ringing sound," Mom said.

Grandpa never knew his parents. His uncle was the only

relative he had, and the man was always sending Grandpa out to beg for food. Grandpa was only twelve when he started working at a blacksmith's shop. "Striking the metal," Mom explained. "He was small and weak. He had nothing to eat. Naturally, naturally ..." A soldier found him passed out in the middle of the road and saved his life by bringing him to a hospital. When Grandpa woke up, he decided he would join the military. It was the military that would introduce my grandparents to each other fourteen years later.

"Actually, your grandpa loved telling stories. He was always agreeing to do things for other people because he felt it was the kindness of others that saved him, but when he wasn't running out of the house to help do this or that, he would sit with me at our dining table. We sat on short stools with a dangling light bulb above us—yes, we had electricity then, we were considered well-off. How do you think I'm so strong? I carried a boiled egg in my pocket to school every morning! Your grandpa loved telling stories. You don't remember because you were too young. He used to cradle you and speak to you for hours!"

When he heard that we were moving, my grandpa said, "You're taking Yuè Yuè from us"—he meant, you're leaving, going to a place I cannot fathom.

I see us at the park, my stroller in front of a concrete fountain, my grandparents sitting side by side. Grandpa smiling into the camera, a small cloth bundle in his arms.

I never got to see my grandpa in person again or hear him tell his stories. In my memories of his video calls, his voice was always muffled, clotted, his focus crumbling like sand.

When he passed, one particular story Mom told me about him played on a loop in my mind: Grandpa driving his combine harvester, his kids running after him through the wheat field, saying, "Come home soon." My mom waving her little arms after him in the field, saying, *come home soon.*

As I'm imagining these scenarios, Emily walks into my parents' room to tell me that she and my dad are going to the hospital. Without looking away from the screen, I tell her that I won't be joining them. I stay behind and click through more albums. The more recent the album, the less I see of myself. I didn't want to be looked at because I didn't look the way I wanted. I thought that I'd rather forfeit memory than remember ugliness. But it's a pleasure to remember.

When I hear our car pull out from the driveway, I hurry downstairs and run out of the house, retracing my steps from this morning back into the woods. The little girl is by the water, just as I had hoped.

It really is a pleasure to remember.

05

I WAKE UP EARLY the next day to count the number of flies on the window. I yawn onto the glass and push my finger through the mist: one fly. I draw a wheel and then the spokes, successfully catching the insect in my silk. My web drips, runs down the glass. Little me wipes the drool from her mouth. Sure enough, I'm the only one who can see her.

Last night, when she came home with me, she headed straight for the basement door. When I realized what she was doing, I blushed and nudged her up the stairs to my bedroom. Excited, she ran all around the room; she ran in circles, locked the door, then, with a hop, resumed running. I was afraid she was going to hurt herself, so I grabbed her, but she started writhing in my arms. Her skin was slick and filmy, and she kept gaping her mouth and gasping silently. "I'll take you back," I said. "I'll tie you to a tree." I spoke quietly. The whole time it felt like a dream. Little Yuè Yuè flipped over and squinted at me. I left her in my room while I went to the washroom to clean my arms. When I came back, she was sitting on the windowsill. "Eh?" She cranked the handle on the window impatiently. "Where's Māma?"

Emily came into my bedroom in the middle of the night. I pulled the covers over myself when I heard our car returning. She stood by the foot of the bed and whispered my name. Little Yuè Yuè almost answered for me, but I pinched her before she could speak. I felt terrible. I threw back the covers to check on her. Little Yuè Yuè let out a great moan when she saw Emily. "Ah! I thought you were asleep," Emily said. She drummed her fingers on my door thoughtfully. "Sorry for scaring you. I guess it's late. Talk to you tomorrow, good night." I almost choked. Little Yuè Yuè was curled into a ball. She made a sound like winnowing rice. I observed her closely, she wasn't that different from a grain of rice herself, small and hard and pale.

Little Yuè Yuè wriggles her fingers under the sun. She's fascinated by the jewellery she found on my dresser. Her delighted face is a handheld mirror I can't stop entering.

I go to the kitchen and hunker down next to Emily at the table. She tells me Mom is doing much better but needs to stay at the hospital to be monitored. The problem is with her pancreas. She has pancreatitis, but there's also something about a growth, a lump, two to three centimetres in length, potentially cancerous, we don't know.

Little Yuè Yuè wriggles her fingers under the sun. Light glints off the silver, the tines of my fork, splintering my eye.

⁂

The door to my parents' room is closed as my dad resumes his work. A shirt jammed in the frame keeps the door from rattling. My dad works from home as a freelance interpreter. When he's not on call, I can hear him repeating after a robot: clemency, chimerical, caraway, collard. Pronouncing after the mechanical voice. Cle-men-cy. Chi-mer-ical. Car-a-way. Col-lard. There is no question that my dad has a larger English vocabulary than me or even Emily, who was born here, yet he cannot understand movies or pick up on song lyrics, and other than the news, which he peruses with Google Dictionary open in another tab, he does not read.

"So what? I have a friend who has the dictionary memorized," my mom once said with a pout. "Front to back, she memorized every definition. I don't know one person who isn't hard-working. What has that done for them?"

"But we always say *you* work too hard," I complained.

"That's because I was born stupid."

"No, you're not!" Emily chimed in. "People always take advantage of you. You have to work ten times as hard! If your English was better, if you could defend yourself ... Yesterday you asked for a 'senior chicken' at McDonald's!"

"Senior chicken. Is that wrong?"

My mom really is hardheaded!

I hear my dad's hoarse voice through the door. "If your shadow falls northeast, is the sun northwest?" "Is a candle made out of wax?" "Are gates and doors similar because they both have openings?" "What do gold and silver have in common?" I hear his fraying heartline.

⁂

The questions—"If your shadow falls ... Is a candle made ...?"—will not leave my ears all day. My dad identifies himself with his employee number. "Everything you say, I will directly interpret."

He repeats what he understands, and what I understand is: your shadow falls, a candle opens, gates and doors are made from silver.

Endearing words spring up—Emily at the door, asking if Dad and I will go on a walk with her. We can see Mars from our lawn, dust rose in the sky. I let the two of them take the lead, following behind with Little Yuè Yuè, who is dragging her heels. I don't know what the matter is with her. She looks at Emily like she's seeing a ghost, now she's looking at Dad weird.

"Bàba's getting old," Little Yuè Yuè says mournfully.

"Really?" I poke her lightly on the forehead. "Are you sure? He looks the same to me."

I tell her she can play on the computer while she waits for us to return from our walk. Her mood immediately lifts and she sprints off. Luckily for me, I can tell my dad is just beginning his story, I haven't missed anything.

"No one wanted to look for me," I can hear him telling Emily ...

"They knew about your yéye. If I was on one side of the road, they would take the other. They didn't dare play with me." Tā men bù gǎn zhǎo wǒ. "But your dad has never lost a fight. I used bricks or switchblades. Once, I even left a line on a boy's neck with my switchblade."

"You almost killed someone when you were a boy?" I ask.

He nods. "My dad, your yéye, kicked me right in the stomach with all his strength."

"Did you cry?"

Even if the story is horrible, I'm grateful for it. Because of it, I come close to seeing my dad as a little boy.

"I ran." Wǒ pǎo le.

"What do you mean you pǎo le?"

"Not my dad, but other people used to tie their children up to beams. We had these roofs with wooden beams from end to end. They'd bind the kid's hands behind their back and throw them up on the rods beneath the ceiling. On roofs. In the summer, boys would have burn marks on their stomachs from the tiles."

We pause at a *No Trespassing* sign at the entrance of the

park. It wasn't there a day ago. A woman can be seen walking her dog up ahead.

"Where we were, it was poor. But even then, not many people did that."

We resume our pace on the sidewalk instead of following the woman's lead and entering the trail.

"My next-door neighbour, we called him Xiǎo Sān. His dad was Zhāng Mázi. He had freckles all over his face, so we called him Mázi," he chuckles. "These are real people."

Our footsteps on the sidewalk echo his words, gentle and solemn.

"Xiǎo Sān's dad would beat him. One day, Xiǎo Sān's teacher scolded him in the courtyard where we could all hear. Pointing at him, he said, 'Xiǎo Sān, watch. I'll tell your dad.' When class was dismissed, Xiǎo Sān went to see a movie. He stayed out really late, then he broke into his dad's workplace—Mázi was in charge of the pesticides in our lián. Xiǎo Sān went home and slept in the bed he shared with his brother, Lǎo'èr. It wasn't long before he started foaming at the mouth." Kǒu tǔ bái mò. "Lǎo'èr turned on the light and put Xiǎo Sān in a wheelbarrow. They only got as far as the school."

My dad speaks with the cool descent of river water, his memories flowing in the sky above us. He recalls the oil lamp for us, how light greased the mud walls. How, when he studied alone at night, he'd hear a sound and think it was Xiǎo Sān's ghost.

94

"Oh, isn't that Xiǎo San's ghost? I felt his soul."

Nà bú shì Xiǎo Sān de líng hún ba?

"I was biking home and he was standing there. He asked to try my bike, but I said I was almost home." Ràng wǒ shì shì ba. "'Your bike,' he said. '*Let me try it.*'"

After he tells Xiǎo Sān's story, my dad starts telling us about another kid from his lián, Lǐ Hua. Unlike most of them, Lǐ Hua didn't get into university. She was taking night classes.

"Lǐ Hua was biking home from class, and there was a turn in the road, so she couldn't see."

Lǐ Hua was studying to be a nurse. Her parents were proud of her.

"They asked your grandpa to do it. People often hired your grandpa for labour because he was strong and because he didn't talk much. I watched him hammer each nail into the coffin. The stink—by then it was many days later, the body was already decomposing. You don't know what the heat was like. Your grandpa said, 'Poor Lǐ Hua,' the smell. Me, your grandpa, eight of us guys total, we covered the top of the grave with soil until we made a mound. Headstones were too expensive. You just built a mound and you visited it, maintained it, added more dirt if you needed to."

"What if it rains?" I ask.

Mosquitoes are starting to come out in the darkness.

"It doesn't rain."

A truck took Lǐ Hua. Prison took her brothers. Xiǎo San

asked to ride my dad's bike before he died. They were all from the same place. My dad opens the door and lets Emily in first, then me, before following us and locking the door. "These are real people, you know," he mutters to himself. "These aren't stories."

⁂

"Little Moon?" I call her. "Xiǎo Yuè, Xiǎo Yuè—Yuè Yuè," I say, patting her head. "You played too much computer. Your eyes are red. Come, let me do your hair."

part 03

01

"DOING?" LITTLE YUÈ YUÈ looks at me in earnest. "I heard frogs singing. I hope we can go catch one. I'm building a pond. When it rains, it will fill up with water."

I sit in the meagre shade of the smoke tree watching Little Yuè Yuè work. She carries on with her digging, struggling with her shovel, grunting, loosening small clumps of grass from the dirt.

"What sound do frogs make in English?" Little Yuè Yuè asks, joining me beneath purple branches. Her shovel lies on its side in the grass.

"You're taking a break already? Hm." I scoot over. "Good question. What sound did you hear?"

She tilts her head in a charming way, pretending to press her ear against a wall of sound.

"Like—*guā guā*." Finger in a quotation, a tadpole, she scratches her nose, suddenly shy. "They say, *guā guā*!"

"*Quack quack* is how we describe the sound ducks make. We say *ribbit ribbit* for frogs. If you listen closely, every animal makes a different sound. Frogs and toads chirp, croak, ribbit ... but birds chirp too. I haven't figured out a way to differentiate their sounds, but I read that some frogs will make a noise like a finger rubbing against a wet balloon, while other frogs have lower calls, like this: *rummm, rummm*. All sorts, monotone calls, raspy calls, clicking sounds, like pebbles striking against each other. And there's likely more than one type of frog in the pond, so you're listening to a chorus."

Having rested enough, Little Yuè Yuè springs to her feet and resumes construction on the pond.

"Big sister!" she calls gleefully. Jiějie! "I remember it now." Wǒ jì qǐ lái le.

I remember it now: wǒ jì qǐ lái: also sounds like: *I tie it up*. Jì qǐ lái.

Jì in this context can also be pronounced as *xì*.

The sound *jì* can mean: to take note, to record; mark; birthmark; to remember; idea, ruse, trick; skill, ability; aid, relieve, help; border between; inside; time, occasion; to be done, to be finished; to cross a river ...

The sound *xì* can mean: a system or series; slender, skinny; small particles; thin and soft, reedy; exquisite, delicate; careful; trifling; young and little, little girl; crack, crevice, chink; gap or rift; loophole, opportunity; ill will, grudge; waterside ritual held in spring ...

"I remember it now. It was like *waah waah*, like a baby—Emily!"

She uses the shovel to shield her eyes from the sun. "It's all over. I can't go on anymore. You have to bury me, Jiā Jiā, heh heh. Come, bury me. Hurry, come on."

Little Yuè Yuè has started calling me by my cousin's name. Jiā Jiā. I decide it's okay.

"Emily was a quiet baby, wasn't she?" I say. "She cried very little."

I remember because my parents always talk about what a good, quiet baby Emily was, but, thinking about my memories of our basement apartment … wasn't there always the sound of crying? I remember it coming from within the walls. Stealthy, rustling sounds I thought were rats until I heard the same sound coming from my mom's back. It came only from her back. I checked her face and saw she wasn't crying. So, what was that sound?

"Forget about it, I don't want you to bury me anymore."

"What's with your change of attitude?"

"Don't talk to me about it." She gazes at the backyard. "I lied to you. I didn't hear any frogs." Her voice has a forced lightness to it.

"I'll take you to look for them. There's a big pond nearby that we can look in. There's lots of animals there. What do you think? If we're lucky, we might see a coyote. If we're unlucky, we'll see teenagers."

"I hate this place. It's so boring."

The rims of her eyes are glowing.

"I hate this place. I hate it. There's nothing to do. I can't do anything. I have no one to play with."

I stay in the shade. There's nothing to say.

"I have no one to play with. Emily is just a baby. She can't play. I hate the kids at school. Do you remember when our teacher made that girl translate for us, and she stepped on our shoes for it? She said, 'You're so ugly, go back to your country,' but we looked the same. I don't even hate her. Everything here is so weird, that's fine. I don't care. I just want to find Jiā Jiā. We can still go to her home, right? Why doesn't Mom take us there anymore?"

"You should come out of the sun."

"I won't. It's nothing—you forget how hot summer gets in China. You forget everything, but I'm starting to remember. Like how I remember the word 'China' in English. Soon I'll replace you. What will you do?"

The hole has filled up by itself. Renew, replace, replenish; recharge with water, even ghosts remember.

I take the shovel from Little Yuè Yuè's hands.

⁎

Emily has been sleeping in my room. She dragged her mattress over and threw it to the ground. I took my pillow and blanket, then lifted the sheets and carried my mattress over to hers.

"Do you remember when we shared a bunk bed?" I ask Emily.

"I was scared of the top collapsing and crushing me." Emily puts her arms and legs up. "This was my plan." She demonstrates for me. "This is how I'd protect myself."

"This is also how goats die," Emily says and bursts out laughing. "With their legs up."

❖

"What are you doing?" Emily's voice comes from behind me as she leans against the deck railing.

"Doing?" I set down my shovel to look up at her, her silhouette glowing in the sun.

"I'm thinking of building a pond here."

"A *pond*?"

"I'm thinking of making a border with those rocks at the side of the house."

"You should fill it in."

"When it rains, it will fill up with water."

"It won't happen like that. You should *fill* it in, before Mom comes home."

"I don't want her to. I don't want her to come here. This isn't our real home. It's time Mom went to her real home and saw her real family. You were born *here*, Emily. How would you know? When things were the hardest for us, you were just a baby, and I had to take care of you. I always had to come home right after school to pick you up from daycare. I couldn't spend any time with my friends. Now you come home late every day. Who knows where you go? You don't love Mom and Dad the way I do. I'm not trying to hurt your feelings, I just mean I love them in a different way. I think ... I love them in a bad way. I'm trying to change. That's why I'm making this pond. I'm going to surprise them. Will you help me?"

It's hard to make out the details of Emily's face.

"Fill it in, Yuè Yuè. We're going to pick Mom up."

Down in my shadow, blades of grass reach up like dark hands. The light shifts—shadows duplicate the original from the inside. The hole I dug duplicates itself from the inside. It has already been filled.

Emily has the idea to buy flowers for when we pick Mom up. Normally, Dad wouldn't want us to waste that kind of money, but today he hands us a ten-dollar bill. "Is this enough?" he asks, leafing through his wallet.

"It has to be—" Emily turns to me. "Right?"

"How should I know?"

My dad parks between the grocery store and the gas station. We head in separate directions: him to the station for a scratch ticket, Emily and I to the store for flowers.

Morning glories are displayed on shelves outside the grocery store. I form a vase with my arched palms, mimicking the funnel shape of the flower.

"Mom told me these are called lǎ ba huā," I tell Emily. "Lǎ ba, like trumpet."

Emily walks past the shelves into the store. The air conditioning raises goosebumps on my skin. We find the bouquets standing in buckets of water.

"Why do they do this?" I point to a blue-petalled daisy. "The dye makes it kitschy."

"Yuè Yuè, let's just get the morning glories. We can't afford this, look—that's more than what we have." Even though she says this, Emily reaches and lifts a bundle of stems from the bucket. "I remember seeing my friends' parents kiss on the lips." Emily holds the dripping stems over her toes. Water falls at a fast pace. "That pond, do you really think they'll let you tear up the backyard?" She sets the bouquet back into the bucket. "Hey, I know what we can get Mom."

Little Yuè Yuè is squatting between two rows of garden shelves, pulling the heads off morning glories. I count the change left over from buying a basil plant and drop the coins with a jingle into Emily's open palm.

"The seeds are poisonous," Little Yuè Yuè says ominously, rolling the petals between her fingers. "I'm making poison. No. I'm making medicine. A *life-saving* cure." She displays her fingertips, the purple bulging from within her skin.

"Oh, that's right. I wanted to tell you about the dream I had last night." I catch up to Emily, who is already halfway across the parking lot. "Actually, I don't remember it. But this morning, it felt like only half of me woke up. In one part of my dream, I was trying to lift something off my face. I was pinching away something, like a clear sheet, pulling it from my face—it *was* my face. I was crying, and I think the tears congealed into a mask, and I was trying to pull it off. It was so awful I woke up, and I was lying on a green pillow. Except my pillow isn't green. I woke up and I was sleeping on a corner of my blanket. The corner was flipped up, and I was lying on the green underside."

"The money wasn't enough?" Dad asks when he sees us.

"We didn't like the flowers," Emily replies.

"Anyway, I waited to see if I would wake up another time, then another."

"Yuè Yuè. Yuè Yuè."

"What?"

"Hello?"

"What?"

"What are you doing? Stop doing that! What's wrong with you?"

"You idiot! You pig head! I'm your older sister, Emily. You don't get to talk to me like that!"

Emily reaches from the passenger seat and grabs at me, grabs something *from* me. "Why would you do that?" She holds the basil plant in her lap, gingerly cradling the leaves. "Why would you do that?"

The undersides of my nails are green.

"Oh! I remember! I remember now. I had a dream that I woke up from a twelve-day coma, having missed nothing except twelve days."

✻

I remember, I remember, car rides with my dad to the grocery store.

I remember, taking the elevator with him into the underground parking garage. The big green dumpsters. The sour smell of rats, dead things, like rotting cabbage heads and thick, coiling pubes, puddles of gasoline.

I remember, pressing my finger into the dents on the side of our car, inspecting the tape over the shattered tail light. Someone had smashed our lights in a McDonald's parking lot. I was standing in the PlayPlace, listening to the sounds of children unsticking their feet from the rubber cushions. I was listening to babies wail. My parents were at the Asian grocery store. I didn't hear anything when the glass cracked. I was standing by the window. I saw a slash of silver. I imagined it. I imagined it was raining.

Dad always asked me to help him pick out a box from the recycling to put our groceries in. "Bàba, look! I found one.

I found a sturdy box. I checked all the recycling and this one was the best. It's sturdy. Heh! Aren't you glad I'm here?"

I asked my dad, I remember, I asked him if I could roll down the window. I had to spin the crank with both of my hands. A light rain fell on my cheek, broke the side mirror into silver drops, silver globes, zhēnzhū bān de fǎnshè, silver reflection. The sky, I remember, was indigo.

I remember how impressed I was, watching my dad drive, turning the wheel smoothly, sharply, the efficiency and ease to that motion, the repetition, releasing the wheel, making a circle: a circle of wind and a circle of melody, a memory, set in place, released by motion.

My dad sang in the car, his voice like blue honey. His singing gave me glimpses of a past life. He told me, "I used to listen to American bands a lot when I was in university. I didn't know what their lyrics meant. I didn't know English then."

The colour of the sky, I remember, was blue like honey.

"Bàba can we take the long way?"

"Gas is expensive, little treasure." Xiǎo bǎo.

I've seen my dad cry. In the car, his singing voice is the closest I have come to touching grief. I watched his jaw drop and the sounds come out.

Our jaws drop—

Releasing fragments of sound—*h-h-h-*

I remember—

"'Hate' is a strong word," my dad says. "*Hate*," he repeats my English. "Are you sure that's the word you mean to use?"

I *hate* trees. I *hate* grass. I *hate* birds. I *hate* the landlord. I *hate* our neighbours. I *hate* small dogs. I *hate* rocks. I *hate* snow. I *hate* the bus driver who refused to let my pregnant mom on for being a quarter short. I *hate* the winter she trudged four hours through. I *hate* snow. I *hate* service workers. I *hate* our neighbours. I *hate* landlords. I *hate* church. I *hate* hospital parking lots. I *hate* grass. I—

"Wrong way," Emily snaps, and I turn around, almost missing the elevator.

I follow Emily and my dad into one of the side rooms and see my mom sitting on a hospital bed, rolling her socks into balls.

02

"THE OTHER WOMAN IS GONE," Mom tells us. "She cried every night. We only had a plastic curtain between us."

Oval tracks encircle the room from above; we rewind the curtain, silver spools of time. My mom sits on the edge of her bed, looking across the room at the other, empty beds.

"In the mornings, her husband always came with a Thermos of zhōu for her. Every morning, he came with zhōu. I could smell the fungal smell through the curtain." She unrolls her socks, which are in balls, like two eggs in the necks of her shoes. She unrolls them and rolls them onto her feet, over her ankles. Rain rolls down the window. She rolls her ear toward her shoulder, cracking her neck.

"I'm so sore. I couldn't sleep well. My entire body is sore."

Dad walks over to the armchair and retrieves Mom's purse. "First, we need to schedule your appointment," he says, checking the inside of the purse.

"I need an MRI."

"You would know better than me. You should be clear about what needs to be done."

"Can we go home?"

"Just wait a minute. Do you have everything? Check the room one last time."

"Do you know what she was in for?" Emily asks. "The woman?"

"Āiyā—she cried so much. I couldn't get any sleep."

"How, I say you—you scatterbrain. You forgot your phone. Aha? See?" Dad points to the pillow. "Always forget this and that." Diū sān là sì de.

"That's it? We can go?" Emily says. "We don't need to wait for the doctor?"

"What doctor? I saw him once and never again. He says he's busy. I guess he can't waste time on small cases like mine."

"But he referred you to a specialist? So, we can just call?"

I turn my back to my family and leave them to their conversation. I walk into the hall in search of a washroom and find a directional sign by the elevator. Evening is drawing near. A few people are sitting around in the waiting area, some asleep, some with their heads bowed. The news is playing from a small, wall-mounted TV above reception. I follow the arrow to the washroom, passing rain-washed windows on my way.

I seem to be the only person in the washroom, but I hear

a crash as I'm washing my hands at the sink. In the mirror, I see one of the stall doors swing open.

"Hello?" I call out, turning around to face the swinging stall door.

I hear no response. Then a call returns, muffled by the sound of rain outside. Someone is moaning on the floor. I rush over, kneeling down, putting my face close to theirs.

"I'm sorry. I don't understand what you're saying. Can I help you get up?" I say as I'm already reaching a hand forward. "I'll go get help. Can I help you get up?"

"Wǒ bù xiǎng sǐ."

I hear the Mandarin and I reel back.

The person's skin is sallow and covered in liver spots. They lift their face and I can see the words dangling from their thin lips.

Wǒ bù xiǎng sǐ—my grandpa says.

I don't want to die.

I reel back, slamming my shoulder into the side of the stall. "I don't want to die," my grandpa says from the washroom floor. The nurses help him to his feet. "I don't want to die." He strains, alone on the washroom floor, until the nurses find him and carry him back to bed.

I reel back, onto the slick grass, green hallway, the light bulbs full of rain, swinging and dripping overhead.

"I saw you in my dream, xiǎo bǎo." My mom sits on the edge of her bed, combing her hair. Little Yuè Yuè puts her hands on Mom's thighs. "You were just a baby." Mom takes the comb from her hair and runs it through Little Yuè Yuè's.

"Māma?" I step toward the girls.

"I've dreamt of Mom," one girl says to me. Her pupils are big and black. Wǒ mèng jiàn mā le. "I've dreamt of Mom," the other girl says. Her pupils are black. "I've dreamt of Mom," the other girl says, and the other one says, "I've dreamt of Mom." Her pupils are small like sesame.

⁂

"Do you remember when Grandpa died? The night before we found out, when everyone was sleeping, I got a text from an unknown number. The text was in Chinese, so I couldn't read it."

"And you didn't translate it?" Emily puts her hands and legs back down, no longer a dead goat.

"When I woke up that morning, I felt like my whole neck was soaked. Because you can't cry in your sleep. You can't really cry, like how you never get to eat the food in your dreams, or if you win the lottery and buy a house, you wake up when you unlock the door, or when you finally find something you've been searching for ... relief or desperation yanks the breath out of you."

It yanks the dream out of me. Everything I try to avoid catches up to me. Yanks the curtains right off the hooks, with tweezers, it plucks every drop of rain from the clouds. Silver strands, white rain, it combs my hair in a black wash down the drain.

"I have Mom's old number," I remind Emily. "So, uncle didn't know."

When I showed Mom the next morning, she accused me of keeping the truth from her. Even though she was asleep when I got the text.

"*Did* you know?" Emily asks.

"It was in Chinese, so I couldn't read it." I flip over onto my side, avoiding Emily's gaze. "But yeah, I recognized enough."

✤

It takes us twenty minutes to walk from the hospital to the spot where my dad found parking. Rain blows sideways in the wind.

✤

Dried chrysanthemums rehydrate in the glass, water yellowing from the top down. We sit around the kitchen table, waiting for my mom's chá to cool.

"Why did he bring her zhōu every day?" I ask.

"Congee is like chicken soup for Chinese people." Emily raises her eyebrows at our parents. "Am I right?"

"Then how come we never have it?"

"Guǎngdōng people drink the most congee," Mom tells us. "My old ma is from the north, but she loves congee. We had it every morning. Girls are taught how to make congee at a young age so that they can be good wives. You want it? I'll make it for you."

"Don't make anything and just rest. They're old enough to feed themselves." Dad nudges the tea over to my mom. "Try it now. You should be able to drink it."

"When I was six, I was making food to bring to my mom at the hospital," Dad says. Emily and I lean forward expectantly. "What can you do? We can't even rely on you to make the rice."

"Mom! We got you something!" Emily runs around the table.

"What is this? Oh! Wow! What is this called?" She reads the tag. "Ba—ba—"

"It's basil."

"Brazil."

"No. *Basil*."

"*Brazil*."

"No—where are you getting the *R* from? It's *ba-sil*."

"Are you going to plant it?" Everyone swivels to look at the backyard when I ask this question.

"You *know* Brazil is a country," Emily mutters under her breath.

The screen door to the backyard is loose from the last time my mom walked into it. I spent half an hour on my knees pinching the mesh back into the frame and managed to get most of it in. Behind this billowing net, our backyard is as square and green as I remember.

I'm the only one at the table. Mom is resting upstairs. Dad is sitting at his computer, searching for information on pancreatic cancer. Emily isn't downstairs or in her room; I assume she's on the phone with a friend again. Lately, she's always on the phone or in her room, chatting on her computer. I wonder what she talks to her friends about.

Maybe I should have left a bucket outside to collect the rain. If we start a garden, we'll need water. The meaning of dreams tends to elude us until we're awake, but by then we've already begun to forget what happened.

Sometimes when you collect a bucket of rain, you'll find ants floating on top of the water the next morning. Black spangled, glistening.

03

EMILY STANDS AT THE TOP of the stone staircase. Everything about her is symmetrical. She untucks one side of her hair from behind her ear and smiles at me. With the camera strap around her neck, she looks just like our dad when he was younger.

I declined my invitation to convocation. I didn't see the appeal in sitting in a rented gown for hours, waiting for my name to be called. And besides, my parents can't come.

"Yuè Yuè, it's beautiful here." Emily looks at the handrail that goes from the stairs to the door. Vines cover the windowsills thickly, leaves like pointed spearheads. Spirelets on the roof; Emily's eyelashes, spirelets beneath her eye. "I want to go here," she says.

"You can go anywhere," I tell her. "You don't have to decide yet!"

When I come back out of the building, I have a big envelope with me. I find Emily in the shade and spin my envelope on one finger like a basketball, making her laugh.

"I've been thinking about Mom's situation. The more I think, the more afraid I get ..." Emily's voice trails off like a small hand-scrawl at the bottom of a page. A web spun in mist. "I saw Mom in my dream. Did I ever tell you? I saw Mom. Like a star, like a star in the water. I was afraid of her."

I find it strange that Emily is speaking to me from the shade. She's standing close to the trunk of the tree, peering at me with one black eye.

"Come with me inside the building. I can show you where I had my classes."

"I can't. I'm too tired. We've already walked a long way." Emily bends to the ground, still hiding behind the trunk.

"Why did you come then?" I can't help but get angry at her.

"I-I can't go. I don't want to go in," Little Yuè Yuè pleads in a small voice.

"Why are you here?" I take her wrists. "Where is Emily?"

"Let me stay. I want to stay here," Little Yuè Yuè begs me.

"Are you done? Is that all?" Emily nods at the envelope in my hands. "That was fast. Do you want to get lunch somewhere to celebrate? I'll take your photo to show Mom and Dad."

"Emily, are you sure you want to go to school here? It's close enough to home that you wouldn't have to move."

"How did you manage the commute?"

"I like trains, and I like seeing the lake. There are people who have it way harder than we do."

"I'm tired."

"We can get lunch somewhere. Find someplace to sit and eat."

"I'm tired. I keep having these dreams. I wake up feeling sad."

"You can tell me about your dreams after we eat."

"What if I forget?"

"Will you really forget so fast?"

"You, Dad, and Mom, you're always looking for something in my dreams. You're always leaving me behind to go look for something or someone. I get so scared that you won't come back"—an accusatory glare. "In my dreams *you* can even fly."

I raise my hands in mock-defence. "Everyone in your dream is you."

"Everyone in my dream is me, everyone in the world is one ... That's why I try to be a nice person. If my friends had to describe me in one word, they would say that I'm nice. It's true. I'm very nice."

Can it be that Emily is more like me than I thought? I never knew she thought this way.

"What are your friends like?" I ask.

She shrugs and reaches for my diploma.

"I don't like them very much."

"Mom and Dad are always saying how they're the only people in the world who'll love us, and ever since we moved to the suburbs, it's like we've become invisible. The suburbs are like a cocoon of trees. Mom and Dad don't have any friends, but it shouldn't have to be that way."

"I feel guilty spending time with my friends."

Emily removes my diploma from its folder and admires it under the sun.

"Congratulations, Yuè Yuè." She looks at me. "You should be proud."

⁂

I wake up to Emily kneeling on the floor by my pillow, knees cushioned on a square of light. "Did I tell you about the dream I had?" she whispers in my ear.

"No, I just woke up."

"Why are you on this side of the bed?"

I flip myself over to look at her. "I woke up at five. I heard someone tossing and turning. I just woke up."

"In my dream, I saw a collapsed building and mourning doves on the fallen beams. The dad bird left to find more materials for their nest."

Mourning doves are lazy birds that will rest on any curb or backyard fence. I don't think I've ever seen one build a nest.

"The baby bird was on its mother's head. They were stacked together. It was adorable. You could fly when we went home. You grabbed your phone and flew off. Somehow, I was able to pry off the top of this window."

I follow Emily's finger to the top of our window frame.

"I had to get my phone ..." I repeat this information.

"I opened this window from the top. You didn't come home until nighttime. When I asked you where you had gone, you said, 'I brought snacks.' I guess you stole two sacks of potatoes." She coils her finger into her palm. "You could have said something before leaving."

Cold water trickles down my face into the sink, which gets grimier no matter how often I scrub it. I pat my face dry with a towel and turn off the washroom light.

In my own dream, I took Little Yuè Yuè downtown. We were surrounded by people wearing leather jackets and wool coats, even though it's summer. Little Yuè Yuè stood close to me. We were on the street, on a curb. Lights had been wrapped around the trunks of the trees; strings of lights hung between the buildings. I felt that there was an argument between us, carried over, but despite her anger, she would touch my elbow, my hand, and I would smile at her.

We were together and we were happy.

⁂

It's a nice, sunny day. Emily and I are walking behind our parents on their daily stroll. Behind the fences along the sidewalk, deep in the construction pits, rain collects blue and minty like toothpaste water.

A neon construction vest hangs from a jutting piece of metal. Emily dares me to reach through the fence for it. I press my shoulder through the square fencing, the bar stopping me at the neck. I drop my arm through the gap and pull, yanking the vest over in one move. At the same time, without Emily seeing, I rip out a handful of dried grass. I chase after Emily with the grass, throwing bits of it at her.

We sprint to the baseball diamond, playing tag, me waving the construction vest around like a victory flag, our circling, almost wasteful steps raising a storm of red silt in the air.

Sometimes, the world has an exaggerated effect that I can't bear—the sodden, saturated world paved with cement slabs and paths of mulch. Like the scales and tunic of a tulip bulb, I can store my entire life cycle underground, but sometimes, in a period of flowering, I feel at ease with the world without having to dull my senses, without having to part with my petals of grief, like life itself can twin my blue base, dual blue heart.

"Yuè Yuè, how can you live so carefree?" Dad asks when he and Mom catch up to us. "You've graduated. We wonder when you will find a job." Wǒ men wèi nǐ dān xīn. "We worry for you."

"When we look at you, you have such an empty expression." My dad's words are lost in the swirl of silt, soft red powder. "You're always so quiet. What are you thinking about?"

What am I thinking about? I'm thinking about how Mom has trouble getting out of bed in the mornings these days. We tell her, "It's time to get up!" but she has to lie there first, rubbing her stomach until she passes gas. Then she says, "I have a bad pancreas!" To which Dad says, "Poor pancreas, made the scapegoat." Bēi hēi guō. And we all laugh.

Bringing me back to the baseball diamond, the silt, Emily says, "On the chance they'll escape an attack by a predator, prey defecate to reduce the chance of sepsis." She pauses, out of breath from running. "I don't know if any of the things I tell you are true."

I feel disgusted. Not because of the idea of feces, but a tooth is tearing through my side, and I may still get away, and already, I need to think about the long survival after.

04

"WHAT DID THE SPECIALIST SAY?"

"A year ago, he said three months."

"Ah, has it already been a year?"

"I do an MRI every three months."

"It's been a year! Look how skinny you are!"

"I can't eat sugar or oily things. I can't have fatty foods."

"Emily! Let Auntie look at you. You're starting university in the fall? Such a good child. Eh? Where's Yuè Yuè?"

"Come in, there's no need to be polite."

"Really, I can't stay."

"There's really no need to be polite."

"You have to come visit me. We're practically neighbours now! I can't stay. I want to, but I can't. You have to come visit me sometime. I can't stay today."

"Are you sure? Come in, sit, have some tea. It's red tea with goji berries. There's jujubes in there too."

"Ah, I brought you something. It's nothing. I hope you'll accept it."

"You do too much. Really, this is too much. You really don't want tea? I'm making lunch soon."

"No, no. I haven't done enough. I've thought about you many times, but I haven't come to see you even once ..."

I roll off the side of my mattress on the floor and kick the last inch of the door closed to go back to sleep.

"Who was that?" When I get up, I glance down from the staircase, past the banister. I see the top of my dad's head as he walks to the living room after locking the front door.

"Lǐ Zhī is a good friend." Dad is careful to avoid tripping on the slippers strewn around the shoe rack. "You said she grew it by herself?"

"They can't finish all this now that their eldest son has moved out."

I go down the staircase. Light pours through the sliding glass door, filling every corner of the living room. Shoe rack, hallway, basement door, the living room with its wooden floors and old leather couch, my family standing at the dining table, bowed and marvelling over two plastic bags.

Emily is on her knees on a dining chair, peering into one of the bags. "They're huge!" She pulls out multiple red lumps from the bag.

"Criticize yourself for your mistakes." My dad begins to put away the tomatoes that Emily has just taken out. "You wake up this late every day! How can you face anyone?"

"Dad's right, Yuè Yuè." Emily looks worriedly at me. "Why do you sleep so much?"

My mom is washing a tomato in the sink with her back to us. She shakes off the water from the tomato and takes a bite. "Oh!" Mom comes over to the table, thrusting the tomato at my dad, who bends his head and takes a bite of the tomato from her hand.

"Can I have a bite?" I ask.

We pass the tomato around, humming and nodding among ourselves, juice dribbles from our knuckles to our wrists; tassels of red hope, around our wrists.

I hear hurried footsteps outside.

"Let's find a time to visit Lǐ Zhī," my mom says and licks from her palm to her fingertip.

It sounds like someone is circling the house, trying to come in.

⁂

Grass shines silver in the field, silver apple, bice green, tall and rustling against the salvaged lumber strewn around the farmhouses. Horses and cows sleep standing with their necks bent into one another. My mom taps the animals on her window and clasps her hands in a prayer pose. The road gets narrower as we drive on.

The air inside the car is breathless, humid, cut into strips of yellow and orange light. We turn onto a private road shaded by trees. Pebbles grind under the car tires, bathing the path in a smoky flame. I shake Emily gently by the shoulder to wake her up.

My dad parks beneath a basketball hoop. The hoop appears to have gone unused for quite some time, for there are leaves caught in the net and thin, barely visible strands of silk on the back of the board. A child's bicycle lies on its side in the grass beneath the hoop, a blue jump rope wriggling on the gravel like the tail of a run-over snake, various other sports equipment, all scattered along the path and by the house.

Lǐ Zhī appears from the side of the house and waves us on. She's wearing a linen shirt and matching pants. Her hair is tucked into a straw hat, which she removes, and on her feet, she wears a pair of strappy sandals. I watch my mom get out from the passenger's side and embrace her friend.

A little boy runs over to us and draws our attention to a row of pots sitting on the patio. Lǐ Zhī introduces her youngest son to us and says, "He's growing cucumbers for a class project." The boy pinches his fingers together. He turns his rosy face up toward Emily and pinches her shirt sleeve.

I ask Lǐ Zhī what her patio is made from. "How grown-up," Lǐ Zhī says to my mom. She turns back to me. "It's a wood-plastic composite. It's recycled plastic."

I knock my knuckles against the planks. They sound hollow when I hit them.

"Easy maintenance." My dad turns his face up to the sky. "I can't imagine it will rain."

"Weather predictions are always unreliable—come in!" Jìn lái! Lǐ Zhī motions for us to follow her into the house.

While the adults head inside, I stay out to look at the shrivelled plants in each pot, my fingers licking the chicken wire, squeezing the fuzzy green nubs. There was one year in elementary school when we all planted flowers and took them home on Mother's Day. My mom placed my flower on the windowsill overlooking the apartment playground. One of the swings had been launched over the top of the swing set, the chain wrapped over and over again on the metal bar. No one came to pull the swing down, so it stayed like that, wrapped, all summer through fall. Then snow came and the ground rose.

Near the back of the patio is a plastic gazebo filled with cushions that appear to have been torn from their seats and tossed into the air. The cushions landed on top of one another on the floor of the patio. Colourful pool noodles stick out from the staggered piles. I kick over the mini-fort on my way in. A birthday banner billows around the support beams above my head. I listen to the wind, the muffled conversation on the other side of the still glass door.

Emily selects a pair of slippers from the bamboo shoe rack and joins me under the gazebo.

"When I was helping Dad sand the deck, I had to wear noise-cancelling headphones," I say to her when she's close. "All I could hear was the beat of my heart."

Emily frees a helium balloon trapped by the patio roof. "Too bad we missed the party," she jokes. We watch the silver balloon crinkle as it flies away.

Lǐ Zhī's backyard is huge. Her garden extends from the side of the house to the back, her only neighbours a group of trees in the distance. They have their own playground set with a double slide and sandbox and a huge trampoline, placed right in front of the trees. Lǐ Zhī's husband is a real estate agent. He was the one who convinced my parents to make a big offer on the house we have now. At the time, there had been three other prospective buyers; when my parents named their price, the other buyers looked at each other and shrugged. They must have thought we were that kind of Chinese.

Lǐ Zhī serves tea from a wooden tray. She passes each of us our own gàiwǎn to drink from. The tablecloth is white with lace edges. From a green cylinder in the middle of the table, I dump out a bundle of wormwood incense that's still sealed with tape.

Chestnut cabinets wrap around the kitchen wall. In the centre of the kitchen is a marble island, where my mom and Lǐ Zhī are cutting and plating fruit. There is a fish tank as well. Like the front yard, the fish tank is littered with children's toys—watercolour markers, action figurines, synthetic seashells—all sitting on a bed of brilliant white pellets. I get up for a closer look, then follow the sound of Emily's voice into the study.

Emily doesn't see me enter the room because her eyes are closed. She moves stiffly across the hardwood floor, her arms outstretched, hands feeling the air. Lǐ Zhī's son darts around the room, whisper-calling to Emily from different corners.

Sketchbook pages cover the table, the floor, in a stack on the piano, drifting off the piano bench; math equations, Pinyin practice; open containers of LEGO bricks; board games, puzzles. I pick a ceramic Dalmatian off the ground and stroke my thumb over its pointy nose. I rub its floppy ears. I hold it.

Lǐ Zhī's son gets excited. "Catch me," he pleads, pinching the bridge of his nose. "*Come catch me.*" He squeezes the words out.

A full-length mirror leans against the wall at the end of the hall. On my way to the washroom, I look into it at myself, at my full self. There are mirrors in the washroom. Tiny oval mirrors, and tiny oval mes crowned with copper spikes; the mirrors framed with copper rims against navy wallpaper. I dry my hands on a towel that feels so soft I worry that I've used a face towel by accident.

I meet Lǐ Zhī's double in the hallway mirror. "You haven't seen my basement yet," her reflection says to mine.

"Come." Lái. "Look at Lǐ Zhī's basement." My mom appears behind us. She has taken her cardigan off. The pink cardigan we spent all morning helping her find. I ask if she's feeling hot. She ignores me and follows Lǐ Zhī into the basement.

"After he went to university," Lǐ Zhī says of her eldest son, sliding a box aside with her foot, "we leave his stuff here." She flips on a second light switch, revealing a home theatre on the other side of the otherwise empty basement. The seats are covered in red leather, and each has its own cupholder and retractable tray. There's a built-in bar at the back. Even in the dark I can see the cherrywood countertops, the glass shelving on the tiled mirrors. The empty glass shelves, layer upon layer of glass.

"My husband did this." Lǐ Zhī chuckles and shakes her head. "It was his idea—*men!*" *Nánrén!*

I can't spot a single crumb or crease on the leather seats of the movie chairs. Some of the seats are still covered in plastic. I can't find a fingerprint on the bar counter. Lǐ Zhī waits with her hand on the light switch for us to finish gawking.

I'm so mesmerized by the silent repetition of Lǐ Zhī's house, its criss-cross reflections, space and emptiness, I almost trip over a bearskin rug, completely missing the hairy mound at my feet. My dad's lips part ever so slightly before he leaves up the stairs.

"Is it real?" My mom bends toward the rug.

"It was a gift."

I get down on my hands and knees to peer into the rug's eye. Obnubilated eye, black eye—this must be the closest I'll ever come to seeing a polar bear's dreams. Yellow nightmare, glass eye. Eternal hibernation.

"Daddy's home, Daddy's home," Lǐ Zhī's son sings from the staircase, and with that Lǐ Zhī flicks off the light.

"Your son doesn't speak Chinese at home?" My dad holds his gàiwǎn over a small dish. Tā zài jiā bù shuō Zhōngwén? He leans forward with his elbows on the counter and waits.

"We don't want to confuse him." Lǐ Zhī tousles her son's hair and tells him to sit. "Here, there are no Chinese children for him to play with."

"How about your eldest?"

"We can only dream!" Lǐ Zhī's husband throws his keys into a small woven basket by the fish tank. "It must be nice having such good daughters!"

We sit together at the table, me next to Emily, my parents, Lǐ Zhī, her husband, and her youngest son. Sunlight fills the kitchen from the big window behind the sink. There is a steamed fish in front of us on the table. "Is that where it went?" I ask. Everyone turns from the dish to the dry tank behind me. Everyone except the boy laughs.

"What?" the boy asks, looking around the table at us. "What?"

Along with the fish, there is broccoli, asparagus, eggplant

stir-fried in oyster sauce, and bitter melon. A fruity yet mellow aroma releases slowly through the water vapour in our gàiwǎn as the tea is passed around the table. The tea is the colour of orange topaz.

"Here, have more fish." Lǐ Zhī pushes the plate toward my mom. "Try some of my sauce." She holds the fish against the bowl with chopsticks and scoops a spoonful of sauce from the side. She then tips the spoon over my mom's plate, the white rice soaking up the brown sauce. Lǐ Zhī picks up ginger and green onions, she picks up a few red chilies, she adds another spoonful of sauce.

Emily, my dad, and I, we all watch my mom. We all look at the fish, which looks back at us from the plate—half-dried pond, soy sauce like mud; chopped scallions, blooming rings of green and white. My mom holds back her hair and slurps from her spoon. She plucks the fish eye and plops it into her mouth.

We watch my mom spitting the fish bones out neatly through pursed lips one by one onto a napkin, lining them up like silver strands of hair.

Before we leave, Lǐ Zhī goes into her garden and picks the rest of her tomatoes, some peppers, and mint. "They'll freeze soon." Lǐ Zhī peers up at the bright sky. "*Chchchch.*" She shoos the air with her hands. "We have more than enough."

"How can we accept this?"—the adults engage in a brief tussle with the vegetables—Zěnme hǎo yìsi?

"*Chchchch*," Lǐ Zhī shoos.

"My stomach is too big," my mom complains in the car. We're waiting at the end of the driveway for the road to clear before turning. Mom buttons her cardigan over her stomach and complains that the cardigan doesn't fit her anymore.

"It's supposed to be worn unbuttoned," I say from the back seat.

"You're going to have trouble sleeping tonight," my dad says. "You had so much sauce. What were you thinking? In front of Lǐ Zhī, what could I say to you?"

"If not because of you, we'd be living in a house like that," Mom says in response. "If you were not so selfish."

We make the turn.

"I don't want to have to drive you to emergency again," Dad says.

A truck appears from behind and swerves past us, forcing us close to the edge.

"Why didn't you honk?" I ask.

"I think it's a good idea," Dad says. "We can have a plot of dirt in the backyard too."

Mom folds her cardigan twice and puts it between her head and the window glass.

"What do you think?" Dad asks. "Plant red pepper ... cucumber ... Didn't we buy basil? We should try growing our own garden!"

Another car swerves past.

"How nice of Lǐ Zhī to prepare those vegetables for us," Dad says.

I glance over at Emily and see that her eyes are closed. Emily's eyes are closed when we turn into our neighbourhood. Closed when we pull up into our driveway. Closed when I take her small wrist in my hand. "Wake up." I circle the back of her wrist with my thumb. "Wake up. We're home."

I hold her.

LIGHT CRYSTALLIZES AND seeds itself over the lake. Long lashes of the willow swaying back and forth in the wind dangle like a piano player's wrists over green keys. I sit facing the water. Wind drops coins into the water; each time a wish is realized, a little bubble breaks on the surface of the lake. Little Yuè Yuè is by my side.

"Why did we come here? Why did you take me to a place like this?"

"We came to see the lake."

I cast my eyes up at the sky. Little Yuè Yuè's palm is like a shapeless cloud, drifting toward the edge of blue. She shakes her head mildly and brings her hand to her chest.

"You're going to leave." She tries to return the gift, the ceramic Dalmatian. "You're thinking of leaving me."

"That's not the reason I brought you here."

Little Yuè Yuè wipes her cheek with the back of her hand. "There's too many little bugs here that I can't see."

"If you say you want to catch frogs, I'll take you."

"No. I've changed. You'll see."

Little Yuè Yuè tries to return the gift once more. "I won't be a bother to anyone."

We sit until sundown, our faces cupping the opal of dusk.

"Dalmatian is my favourite type of dog."

"See, you haven't changed."

The water is lepidolite. We let it well up between us.

"You don't have to stay around the house all the time. A year—a year is a long time. It's been over a year. The growth on Mom's pancreas hasn't gotten any bigger since her last MRI. Her checkups are every six months now instead of every three. There is no treatment, no diagnosis. Her doctor said that she can have the growth surgically removed, but Mom declined." When the wind quickens and waves break out over the surface of the lake, does it not look violent? And yet, is it not benign? "You'll wear yourself out if you stay."

"I want to go home. I-I want to be near her." She plucks a coarse blade of grass and pulls it taut between her thumbs. "I want to be with her forever."

I only nod.

She tries whistling with the grass, and when she fails to make any music, she shreds the blade into ribbons.

"You're only wearing yourself out."

"Jiā Jiā could do this."

"Why don't you call me by my name?"

Little Yuè Yuè tries once more to whistle with a blade of grass.

"You have too many names. Even you don't seem to mind what people call you."

It's true. I have my legal name, my English name, and my xiǎo míng Yuè Yuè, which is what my family calls me: a childhood name, a pet name. Yuè Yuè, every month, every moon, the current, the present.

"It doesn't matter what people call me as long as they recognize me for who I am. You can call me Jiā Jiā, but don't you want to see your cousin again? See the real Jiā Jiā?"

"See the real Jiā Jiā ..." Little Yuè Yuè spreads her fingers over her face. "But I can't leave Mom's side."

"It's my fault for making you come with me. It's because of me that you're pinned to one place. You've helped me remember many things—take off your shoes and your socks and put your feet in the grass."

The grass tickling her feet seems a little damp. She puts her hand on my throat—*See, it's cold*. She giggles. "Let's stay here a while longer."

We lean back onto the grass, watching the willow sway, the light from the train station flickering behind us like a distant campfire.

"I want to apologize to Emily for being a bad sister."

"You'll make her sad if you say that."

"Sometimes I can't stand seeing her happy."

"Can you see me? It's really dark now. Look at me—can you see my face?"

"Let's go home."

"No, you can't see me. It's too dark. We're a part of nature now."

"Don't walk that way, you'll drown."

"Why would I drown?"

"The water's too cold."

"Why would I drown if I know how to swim?"

"Listen—that's the sound of the train. Hurry and put your socks on."

The steps on the train are slippery. I gaze into the coach for some time before choosing my seat.

"What is it?" Little Yuè Yuè is sitting opposite to me. I move across to sit next to her. "What's wrong?" I ask her.

"I left it on the grass. That little doggy. I forgot about it."

"Oh."

"Stupid. I'm so stupid."

"It's okay. I stole it anyway."

"I really loved it. I loved it so much, and I forgot it in the grass."

"I know you love it very much." I stroke her hair. "I know," I repeat. "I know how much you love it." Little Yuè Yuè hiccups in my arms. "I know you love her very much. You love them all very much. You really, really love them."

She laughs. "You're very funny."

I laugh with her. "You *are* troublesome. Are you done now?"

"You'd better apologize to Emily."

"I will."

"I'm worried about her."

"It's funny to hear you say that. You're a worldly-wise person. You've seen a lot of the world."

"You should give this to Emily." Little Yuè Yuè thrusts a fist toward me.

"Where was that? Where did you find it?"

"It was in my sock."

"She won't want anything that's been in your sock."

"I used to have a lot of fun with Emily. Now that you mention it, ever since we moved to Canada, we haven't been able to travel. Emily hasn't seen any of the world, but every summer break, I'd take her out to the park or the library. I'd take her around and I'd play with her."

I take the ceramic Dalmatian and slip it into my pocket.

"Dalmatians are Emily's favourite type of dog," Little Yuè Yuè says.

"She likes whatever you like because you're her older sister."

"No, I'm not. I'm only twelve." Little Yuè Yuè sounds very pleased with herself. "I was only six when I came here, now look how old I am!"

"Your English has improved significantly. But your Mandarin has grown worse."

"Mom and Dad signed me up for Chinese school, but it was for Cantonese. It was so embarrassing!" Dramatically, with her head held in the crook of her elbow, she says, "I didn't know anything!"

"You have time to put your socks on."

"It doesn't make a difference to me, but I'll put them on."

I glance at my reflection, blurred and doubled on the evening glass.

Little Yuè Yuè has become transparent, silver. I find glimpses of her in fresh water, in mirrors, on fish scales and fins. In Emily's face, fragments of light in Emily's eyes—even though she looks more like Dad, and I look like Mom. Yuè Yuè, the word for "moon," uttered twice. Out of her small mouth: silver repetition. Out of the sky. Out of memory. Silver repetition.

Out of relief or desperation: out of want: out of hope.

Inside my dreams, I'll repeat my memory, and everyone in my dream is you.

part 04

01

AT SEVENTY-FIVE, MY GRANDMA, 外婆, can no longer reach her toenails. 外公, I'm told, used to trim her toenails for her, but when he passed away, 外婆's toenails grew too long and cut into the skin of her adjoining toes.

My grandparents lived with my uncle's family—they raised my cousin, and for a short time, they raised me. Now my cousin takes care of 外婆 whenever she can. She accompanies 外婆 to the street market before school every morning. They buy freshly brewed 豆浆, sticks of 油条 still sizzling in their paper bags, and various pastries filled with 红豆沙. My cousin wears a navy skirt and polo shirt and sheer white stockings. She stands obediently by 外婆's side and watches as the vendor dips a long ladle into a large vat before pouring the 豆浆 into a plastic bag and twisting the edge of the bag into a knot, some of the milk flying as the bag spins. At least that is what I like to imagine—that people still wait in lines for fresh 豆浆 in the busy wood-smoked streets, the curb hidden entirely by bike carts with pages of newsprint billowing from their sides; that a large 馕 costs two yuan (about forty cents), 五毛 for a small 馕, the rounds of dough curled at the edges and stamped with a laced pattern of holes, sprinkled with black onion seeds and chopped garlic; that my 外公 is taking his midday nap on an indoor balcony under a decorative grapevine whose grapes are firm and plump year-round, and when we spill through the door like warm light, he'll open his eyes.

Sitting in nothing but her underwear on a metal folding chair, my mom would call twelve hours into the future. She'd flex the plastic calling card in the palm of her hand while she sat with her head bowed, listening. Calls were expensive. My parents allowed themselves one call per month, and each call lasted roughly five minutes. I stood next to my mom when she made her calls. The straps of her polyester bra would slip off her shoulders, and I'd pull them back up for her. I couldn't hold conversations with my limited Chinese, so I stood there, fixing my mom's bra straps, plucking her silver hairs, whispering messages into her exposed ear. When she put the receiver down, she would always tell me, 外婆说她很想你 (Grandma says she misses you!), and sometimes, even with the phone hung, I could hear 外婆's crinkling laugh through the line.

As I got older, I stopped standing next to my mom during those monthly phone calls. The calls always began with asking about each other's health, then the children's schooling, before moving on to more trivial things, like comparing market prices, the weather, and different ways to 养生 (stay well). Still, my mom would put the receiver down and say, 外婆说她很想你 And I would never fail to respond, 我也很想她—but those repetitive words, phrases, they echoed forth from me like paper boats, weightlessly. Language proved unable to ensure materiality. Even when video calls became possible and my 外婆's face appeared before me, wrinkled like an orange left in the sun, I could no longer tell which one was imaginary: the 外婆 in my mind, the old image I had to repeatedly conjure, or the image on the computer screen, frozen and lustreless.

Melancholy scalded me from the inside. I opened my mouth and only steam came out. So, I stopped appearing, and those twelve hours stretched into twelve long years.

In those twelve years, I was plagued by dreams of the future. I dreamt that my 外公 died of a heart attack. I dreamt that my 外婆 bent over the flour sack in the kitchen, unable to reach her toes, and wept.

✻

I laid my head on my mom's lap, facing her knees, so she could help me 掏耳朵 (clean my ears). I watched the wax pool on her knee. She scooped mountains out of me. I felt a boulder dislodge and wind breeze through my ear canal and water falling out. When she finished, she blew over my ear, her breath an arch, a rainbow. She patted my back for me to get up, and I cleaned off her knee with a tissue.

Above the telephone, there was a poster of the world map held up with tape. I knew from my dad that the country shaped like a chicken was China. My mom's back was pink where the band of her bra dug into her skin. The buttons on the phone shone forth in the early light, and I could hear the faint sound of the dial tone like footsteps passing back and forth. "They must have already gone to bed," my mom said. With a sigh, she let the receiver fall.

⁂

The sea scoffs at 精衛 for trying to fill it with twigs and pebbles, saying that she will never be able to fill it even in a million years, to which 精衛 says, then I will spend ten million years, I will spend one hundred million years.

Jīngwèi drowned while playing in the Eastern Sea and was transformed into a bird. She uses her beak to pick up small pebbles and twigs to drop into the sea; even after metamorphosis, flying backwards, she'll do whatever it takes to prevent someone else from suffering her fate.

The sea scoffs at 精衛, to which she says, I will be ten million birds, I will be one hundred million times transformed.

⁂

I looked up at the world map, at the country shaped like a chicken, at the sea—through the receiver, the sound of lapping water flooded my ears.

I inherited 精衛's spirit. Every time I visit the lake, I linger by the shore with a pebble in my hand, looking out at the quiet horizon where the gulls are silver, immortal. In *my* life, water is what keeps me from my 外婆, but water is like memory: it swells with time. I hope not so much to fill the deep-blue abyss but to touch briefly its surface.

It fills me with shame that I have never cupped my 外婆's blistered heel in my palm while clipping her toenails into a low toilet, that I have never known the cooling smell of salve on her skin, never had to down a giant bowl of her 绿豆汤 every morning, prepared with snow fungus, adzuki beans, goji, and dried lily.

What right do I have, by a bird's wish, to go to her in my human form?

✼

One morning, I walked in on my mom having a family video call on her laptop at the kitchen table. She was remarking that the maples growing in our neighbourhood were in bud. I picked up the kettle that had just come to a boil and brought it over to the table.

A blue square on the laptop screen held my 外婆's face.

It was my first time seeing her face in years—years that I had let grow, thick and fungal, between us. Never had I felt more deprived, than in that moment, seeing her face again. Never had love felt more impossible.

I felt as if all the good things had been kept from me. And yet—her face upon seeing mine broke into a smile so wide it wrinkled like an orange left in the sun. 精衛's spirit was in my 外婆's wrinkles, the same spirit traversed one thousand transmigrations. In her mouth, my 外婆 would carry a stem of lotus, *connection to origin*, sometimes a willow branch, *to bend and not break*, and even sprigs from peach trees, *the divine tree of immortality*. I started doing what I could, bringing pebbles and twigs.

We dropped words between us, simple words we both could understand:

你好 (hello) she said.

你好 (hello) I said in return.

The language I thought had died in my throat dropped like a star in the water. Sound, echo, mood, the cold tide, flowing. Every day for a thousand years, 精衛 said to the sea: 你好 (pebble) 你好 (twig).

⁂

I cupped the image of 外婆 and began trimming the years. Each nail was a different phase of the moon. I cupped the heel of her words and traced their curves.

We are unable to communicate anything. We never ask each other questions. 外婆 weeps for 外公 when her toenails grow too long, when she comes back with breakfast and the grapes hanging green and purple from the skylight are forever ripe but never sweet.

But even in these times, 外婆 can still step out onto the colourful and crowded streets, into the smoke of char-grilled meat, the scent intoxicating yet meltingly soft. She can negotiate the price of fruits, tea, cloth; fill a paper cone with a scoop of chilies, a scoop of cinnamon, then cumin, saffron, whatever she wants to season that night's dinner. She can stop and watch vendors cut melons into scarlet wedges with tapered knives, buy dried figs the size of marbles. On the ground, men are beating copper bowls; she can bring home a handcrafted pitcher if she wants, but her hands by that point may already be full.

外婆 seldom makes trips outside their apartment now that my cousin can't accompany her (my cousin has long left for university), but when she does go out, even now, she returns with the same 豆浆 brewed fresh, a bag of fried dough sticks.

✻

The video call ends. The house is quiet, and I can hear the kitchen tap running. When was the last time I let my mom clean my ears? When did I stop plucking her white hairs for her? How come I drew my hand away, as if burned, when she asked me to massage her back?

I join my mom by the sink and thrust my hands under the tap before she can shut the water off. When I finish washing my hands, she passes me a bowl of green beans and we get to work, standing side by side. The crisp sound of snapping beans echoes around the bowl of the sink.

Snap-snap-snap—sound skates the silver rink; silver snaps fill the bowl.

❋

Maybe the myth is misremembered—maybe the sea doesn't scoff at 精衛. Maybe the sea, lapping hopelessly, only wants to touch the pebbles at the shore again, and again, and again.

02

I'M FILLING EVERYONE'S cups with water from the kettle when my mom announces that my cousin is flying to Canada for a visit. In my shock, I spill hot water on Emily's wrist. Little 月月 is the first to respond; she drags Emily over to the sink by the elbow and runs cold water over her burn.

I recently learned the characters for my cousin's childhood name. Most people who read her name (茄茄) will call her by the more common pronunciation "qié" (eggplant), instead of "jiā." I never knew this. My inability to read characters, my reliance on pinyin—this entire time I was on a completely different page from everyone else.

Mom hurries to bring Emily a bag of frozen peas. When she presses it against Emily's wrist, the clip falls off the bag with a snap and small, green, shivering creatures cascade down the drain.

"I'm so tired," Emily says. She pulls her wrist out from the water for us to inspect. Her skin is bright. "When the water isn't running over my burn, it hurts so much." With a wince, she thrusts her hand back under water.

Emily was six when she met 茄茄 for the first time. Six years had passed since we moved to Canada. I was twelve. I don't know what shocked my cousin more: seeing me or Emily.

⁂

I learned about migration from watching geese lift, one after the other, into the grey sky. A skein of geese, in cursive, like lyrics, expressing spring emotion. When the geese returned, I knew my classmates would leave.

My classmates would embark on their mini-migrations: to the cottage for a month, to their trailer, to somewhere tropical I'd never heard of, to see their grandparents *back home*.

When they asked me what my plans for the summer were, I'd fall quiet. They averted their gazes from me as if they had caught me molting. As if I had lost all my feathers in a simultaneous molt, rendering me flightless.

⁂

With all my friends gone for the summer and my parents away at work, I was left to babysit Emily. I took her to the playground every day. We shot oblong nuts at black walnut trees to see who could knock down more nuts, our hands stained by green husks and smelling of pine and citrus. We pushed my rickety bike through fields of red clover and took turns riding down the hill. We fell on our backs in the grass and plucked the clover heads off their hairy stems, sucking on the petals: a tinge of sweetness mixed with sweat. We ate elm samaras, placing the flat, light-green disks on our tongues, closing our eyes and savouring the softness.

On sweltering days, we sought refuge inside the small library at our local mall, sharing one chair in front of the computer while we played flash games until our time was up. We'd drag stools directly next to the bookshelves and stack a tower of books on the carpet by our feet, pulling and reshelving as we went from one end of the library to the other. I loved reading fairy tales, while Emily preferred books about bizarre facts. No one ever bothered us.

My classmates returned with interesting snacks for me to try—sakura mochi Kit-Kats from Japan, jelly sticks from Hong Kong. Once or twice, to show my gratitude, I even led some of them to the elm tree where I got my seeds, pointing up at the green clusters and blushing.

✳

A sequential molt is when birds lose their feathers one at a time. Waterfowl lose their feathers all at once in a process called simultaneous wing molt. New feather shafts (called pin feathers) are highly sensitive, and when damaged, they can bleed profusely. During this molting time, geese will stay on waterways such as lakes or ponds to have a safe resting place from predators. Geese undergo an annual molt, while most ducks undergo two molts.

They leave home to survive the winter. They return to breed, to survive the future.

⁎

On my tenth birthday, after I had helped my mom tidy the entire kitchen and living room, I brought up flying. At that moment, the front door unlocked and my dad came in. He was home early from work, holding his hand in a weird way. I had only to look into his feverish eyes to know that I would not be seeing my grandparents that year.

Eventually, my dad's hand healed and he quit his warehouse job. By the time my twelfth birthday came around, I was happy just to have my family around the table and healthy, so I was taken aback when my mom let slip with a sigh, "My parents are finally going to meet Emily."

"What about me?" I had to ask.

Before my mom could say anything, my dad slammed his

chopsticks down. "Didn't we discuss this beforehand?" He glared at my mom, who looked away from me.

"I only ask for this *one* thing for my birthday ..."

My parents were yelling at each other across the table.

"Please." I spoke in a quavering voice. "I'll never ask for anything else."

"Hush!" my dad scolded me. "Each year you get older, but have you changed at all?"

I turned to my mom, only to find her glaring at me. Naturally, I began to cry.

"You're crying like a baby. Really, aren't you ashamed of yourself?"

"Mom!" I exclaimed, covering my face and sobbing miserably.

Emily followed me to the washroom. "I hate you to death," I seethed—我恨死你了—before slamming the door in her face. If it weren't for Emily, I'd be the one flying home. If it weren't for her, Mom could've taken me back years ago.

Emily repeated my name over and over again, her gentle voice curving upwards from the space between the floor and the door. I stopped crying. I was calm. I looked at myself in the mirror and saw black spots floating everywhere in my vision. I looked at my eclipsed self behind those floating dots.

※

Dad saw us off at the airport. He stood smiling by the gates and gave us a small wave. The floor was so carefully polished that my dad's reflection spilled forth from his feet—light bounced off the pool of him, wetting my eyes. I dropped my bag and ran to him and grabbed tightly to his waist and wouldn't let go.

Our flight had an overnight layover in Beijing, a city I had never been to. My mom had a friend who was there on sabbatical, who was kind enough to find a place for us to stay. The room he arranged for us was no larger than a cubicle and had only one cot for the three of us to share.

"Hurry up and get some rest," Mom said with her hand on the telephone. She was making calls to our family to let them know when we'd be arriving by train.

The air in the room felt obscure and oppressive. My legs were red and itchy where they had touched the mattress. Emily was breaking out in hives. I touched the rosebuds on her neck and she rocked forward, crying out. Mom put the chain on the door, then stuck her shoe between the door and the frame to let in the night breeze.

Another, shorter flight later, we arrived in the city where I was born, but all I can remember about that visit is sharing an umbrella with Emily while we stood outside a hotel dining hall that would not let us in. I remember looking through the glass doors at the buffet-style reception; there were large oval cloches and oyster plates, sugar bowls raised on four feet, silver-plated creamware, crystal swan napkin holders, and on every table, a revolving epergne. I stood awkwardly while my mom waved the breakfast tickets she had paid for. She was being very loud, and people were starting to shoot us dirty looks. It dawned on me that the city had forgotten us. I remember my futile protests. "I don't want to eat here." What I meant was that the restaurant was clearly too fancy for people like us, but my mom had her pride to protect.

For all that bickering, we were on the train and leaving the city that very afternoon. My mom warned us not to tell anyone where we were from. "They assume everyone who comes from overseas is rich. If people find out you're foreigners, they will kidnap you and ask for money." Mom held our boarding passes out of reach until she had our promise.

To my excitement, there were bunk beds on the train: one against each side of the cabin with a table between. There weren't any doors. I scampered up onto my bunk and leapt from the bed onto the table, then climbed back onto the bunk and leapt again. My mom tried to catch me mid-fall, fishing for my leg with a hooked arm. I kicked out and knocked over a Thermos—the lid flew off with a clatter and disappeared beneath the opposite bunk. I took my chance and dashed into the corridor.

Hearing the ruckus, an old woman poked her head out of her cabin and asked me to join her. "Is that your sister?" The old woman looked past me at Emily, who had followed me there. Knowing vaguely about China's one-child policy, I felt like I had to provide an explanation for why I had a sister. I blurted without thinking, "We're Canadian!"

我们是加拿大人

"Oh, Jiānádà." The old woman clasped her wrinkled hands together.

We spent the next few hours in the old woman's cabin, eating 话梅 and spitting out the pits, my saliva dark purple and salty on the napkins. The old woman showed us rivers flowing between the cliffs of her calluses and taught us how to read our own fortunes from our palms. "Aie!" Emily squealed when the old woman tickled her hands. "Aie! Aie!" Even my mom had to laugh at the sound of those squeals. "Emily will have a long life," the old woman decreed. She then took my hand palm-side up and, frowning, clawed my skin with her index finger. The old woman was just about to say something when my mom grabbed my hand from her and hid it under the table.

My uncle, 舅舅, picked us up from the train station in a yellow Jeep. He was working as a car salesman, so he always had access to nice cars. We drove with the windows down on orange roads soft with sand. No one was wearing a seat belt. I asked many times if this was legal, but no one took my concern seriously. Eventually, I gave up and stuck my arm out the window. Sand swirled along my forearm, tickling the hairs. It seemed like we were barely moving. Time itself was yellow. I opened the door.

Sand hissed up from the ground. Sand spun in a coil, bolted up.

The wind was so loud I couldn't hear my mom yelling at me to close the door. She reached over me and grabbed the handle, slamming the door shut. 舅舅 directed his full attention to me for the first time since we'd arrived, holding my gaze in the rear-view mirror. Sand hummed against the sides of the car. The radio buzzed. My 舅舅 was in high spirits despite what had happened. My aunt, 舅妈, he informed us, had purchased bathing suits for everyone ahead of time—we were going to a spa.

外婆 met us inside the change room, her curly hair already tucked away in a swim cap. She squished me against her breasts for a long suffocating hug before passing me a bathing suit. I rubbed the cheek that she had pinched and wandered off to find a private corner of the change room. I was sure that my 外婆 had become shorter.

I changed quickly, then waited for the others on a bench. Beautiful women drifted around me in white towels. They swished around like 仙女; like fairies, they wafted through the steam. Their bodies smelled like feathers and sandalwood, yellow guava, jasmine alps. They moved like a forest of willow trees, weeping and silver.

舅妈 led my mom to the baths while 外婆 took Emily and me in the opposite direction. We followed 外婆 past a row of potted fan palms to a sparkling blue pool. On the floor were strips of hot stone, the walls were painted in neutral colours, and there were no windows. 外婆 squatted on her haunches by the side of the pool and started blowing up inflatable arm bands for Emily. I rested my elbows on the ledge and leaned my head back, paddling the water. We were the only people there. I closed my eyes and 外婆's breath slithered into my ear like sand.

The bathing suits 舅妈 had picked out for us had frilly tutus that spread above the water when we jumped in the pool. Light reflected off the sequins on our tutus like fish scales. Emily bobbed up and down, held afloat by inflatable arm bands. When I called to her, my voice echoed back like hoops.

It was late afternoon when we left the spa. Heat drenched us the moment we stepped outside. My skin was once again covered with a fine layer of sand.

Children travelled in groups on the street. I was busy admiring their uniforms—pleated skirts, trousers, white shirts with colourful sleeves, some of the children wearing red sashes around their necks, almost all the girls with their hair in pigtails, like me, and all of them sporting their school badge proudly below their collars.

茄茄 squeezed the remaining water from the tips of my hair then touched the tops of my shoulders where my shirt was damp. "I wish I could have gone swimming with you, but I had school," my cousin said. I noticed that she was wearing a red sash around her neck as well.

茄茄 smiled easily, as if it were natural for me to be outside her school. She still had her backpack on when she pulled me in for a hug.

外公 was standing next to my mom. "Grandpa!" Emily yelled, before throwing herself at him. "I love you, Grandpa!" She threw herself at 外婆. "I love you, Grandma!" Only with 茄茄 did she hesitate, chewing on her thumb and glancing at our mom for permission. "That's your cousin," mom said. 表姐. She thought about it for a second and said, "That's your *sister*, Emily," because 姐姐 was a term Emily understood.

On the walk back to their apartment, I pulled Emily aside and asked whether she really meant what she said. "How can you love them?" I asked. I pressed her to answer me. We had purchased plastic bottles of frozen Sprite on our walk and now were cracking the bottles against the pavement to loosen the ice.

We sucked on the trapped glaciers, shaking loose chunks of ice onto our tongues. My family no longer lived in the countryside—they hadn't in years. The air was cool and splintered with glass. Watching the fluffy white clouds in the sky, I already knew time was passing. I stepped back in from the balcony. On the screen door were yellowish marks left by sand.

✻

茄茄 took me to meet her school friends at a café. A bunch of them were sitting in wicker swinging chairs, texting on their flip phones. It was the weekend, so they were dressed casually in sundresses and graphic tees. They greeted me generously, each taking a turn to pat my head.

"My sister's back from Canada," 茄茄 said with pride.

Everyone ordered their drinks, and when it was my turn, I blinked at the menu, using my finger to point at the pictures and stumbling over my words. The person taking my order demanded that I speak faster. 茄茄 and her friends jumped to my defence, getting up and huddling around me. "She's not from here," 茄茄 explained. "She doesn't understand."

I felt responsible, though nothing had happened. I wanted badly to impress the older kids. I thought they would ask me to say something in English, but they returned to their conversations about people I'd never met and shows I'd never watched. I could tell that they pitied me. I couldn't read or write. I could barely communicate. I knew nothing and no one. I couldn't even go anywhere without 茄茄 holding my hand.

That night, I slept between my grandparents on their hard mattress and my thoughts moved to my dad. While watching dust particles float in the moonlight, I thought about whether he had started his workday, what he was going to have for dinner, and whether he was still going for walks in the park; meanwhile, 外公 was snoring loudly next to me.

外公 was eight years 外婆's senior, and by the time of my

visit, his activities were limited to sitting in front of the TV or sunbathing by the large windows in the living room. But despite not being able to accompany us to most places, he was full of ideas on where to go. It was his idea that 外婆 cook lamb for dinner, even though he didn't have any teeth to chew the meat with. (Emily screamed each time 外公's dentures came out. I couldn't believe it either, seeing the gleaming strip of pink above the teeth.) So 外婆 woke me up early and 舅舅 drove us thirty minutes from his apartment to a pasture.

The unpaved road was bumpy, dented with memory. Wind rolled like waves on the top of the car. I saw Mongolian yurts in the field and lambs grazing by the water and hills so round they seemed to be filled with dreams not yet held by any sleeping mind. That night, I had the best 抓饭 of my life. 外公 picked out the mutton from his bowl for me, and from my bowl, I picked out the mushiest pieces of carrots and the soggiest raisins for him.

"Can you give me the recipe?" My entire family laughed when they heard me asking my 外婆 this question. "Zhuāfàn is my bàba's favourite," I explained.

"Yuè Yuè!" 舅舅 called my name. "How long do you think your bàba lived in China? You think he hasn't eaten way more delicious foods than you have?" 也太小看他了吧! "You underestimate him!"

What I wanted most while I was there was to play with 茄茄 the way we used to, but she spent all her time doing schoolwork in her bedroom with her door locked. Occasionally, she'd go to the café to see her friends, but even then, they'd just be studying together. I tried to recreate my early adventures with 茄茄 with Emily, but Emily was undergoing a great change—her chest, neck, and both arms were covered in pink blotches. No matter what creams we used on her or how many baths we gave her, the hives would not get better. I stayed with her to see what she would become.

I told Emily she was turning into a lizard just to frighten her. She was having a particularly hard time breathing that day, and we ended up having to take her to the hospital. While we were waiting for the doctor, my mom used the pay phone to place a long-distance call to my dad. At the sound of his voice, both Emily and I started crying.

茄茄 did not come with us to the train station to say goodbye, and Emily's allergies went away naturally upon our arrival in Canada.

茄茄 either hugged me goodbye by the door of her apartment, or the door was where she greeted me when I arrived. 外公 was at the door too.

Or 外公 was asleep on a chair by the window.

I can't remember.

✬

"By morning, you'll forget the pain," I tell Emily.

I convinced her to take a walk in the rain to distract her from her burn.

"That's just like us." My dad points to a flock of geese. Lacking in numbers, the sides of the V-formation are uneven.

One of my wishes is to fly with my entire family. My wish is for us to be able to afford four plane tickets at one time. I wish that my parents could fly home together; Emily and I are old enough to take care of ourselves, but if my parents both left for a month, we would not be able to help pay the bills.

"Do you think they're lonely?" my dad asks in a faraway voice.

"The little sister goose is probably annoyingly talkative."

"*You'd* be that one." Emily shakes my shoulder from behind. "The straggler."

"If *you* hadn't been born, our V would be even."

"Slowpoke."

"Idiot."

"You ruined the formation."

"*You* ruined the formation."

"Both of you be quiet," Dad says—and with a wink—"Listen to your leader."

We reach the end of the path and hoist ourselves onto a raised drain cover to observe the ducks in the pond. Ducks glide along the chilled edges of the pond with their necks tucked into their back feathers, undisturbed by passing cars. Emily leans against one side of me, Little 月月 on the other.

"My wrist is breathing." Emily pulls back her sleeve. Steam rises from her wrist. The hot water left a mark like lightning across her skin, spreading from the wrist bone, tiny quivering streaks.

The ducks rest lazily on the pond, going nowhere. The ducks are awake, picturing fish.

If they don't fly, they will never strike the sides of buildings, mistaking the glass for sky.

03

THIS MORNING 李枝 (Lǐ Zhī) stops by our house with bags of roots and vegetable scraps in the trunk of her SUV. After leaving the roots on our porch, she gets back behind the wheel and pulls out of our street, followed by my parents in their car. They all return an hour later, assisting each other with cedar planks, wire fencing, and sacks of soil and fertilizer.

Light crinkles bluely in their early eyes. With 李枝's help, my parents decide on the location of the garden and begin construction in the backyard, my dad pushing over the manual lawn mower from our small shed. They pace the perimeter of the yard with arms folded behind their backs.

Emily curls up on the couch indoors with a book on her knees.

Sliding sunlight on the bare arm of a deck chair; a saw slides across a plank of yellow wood. Yellow sawdust, silver nail. Raised garden beds erected at the end of the yard and filled with soil.

The only work left, it seems, is the roll of wire that needs to be cut and coiled around the boxes to keep out wild rabbits.

Dad reads this to us from his journal:

"1981-11-18 (阴)。早晨，我站在门口吃饭时，被三个鸡子吸引住了：一只子鸡是老母鸡，另一只是大一点的母鸡，另一只是比两个母鸡都大的小鸡。开始，老母鸡独自埋头在槽里吃着，另一只母鸡看见，立刻赶去，头刚要伸进鸡槽，不料被那母鸡发现，它用威胁的声音叫着，双眼盯着去的母鸡，这母鸡猛一惊，呆呆地也一动不动地注视着老母鸡，它们相视了几秒后，老母鸡就不管这母鸡了，又吃了起来，这母鸡满以为无事，立刻吃了起来，不防老母鸡上前就啄它的脖子，它就立刻吓得掉头就跑，碰巧，遇见了正要老吃食的小鸡，它好像要拿小鸡出气，小鸡不知怎么一回事就挨了打，只有那胜利者、强者老母鸡、津津有味地吃着。

"1981-11-18 (cloudy). In the morning, as I stood at the door to eat, my attention was caught by three chickens: one was an old hen, the other was a slightly bigger hen, and the other was a chick that was bigger than both hens. At first, the old hen buried her head in the trough to eat by herself. The other hen saw and immediately rushed over. Right as the hen was about to stick its head into the trough, the old hen unexpectedly noticed it and cried out threateningly with a glare. The other hen was shocked and stared stupidly back at the old hen without moving. After they stared at each other for a few seconds, the old hen lost interest in the other hen and started eating again. The hen thought there was no longer anything to worry about and quickly began to eat. The old hen rushed over and pecked its neck. The hen ran off in fear. Coincidentally, it ran into the chick, who was about to eat. To let off steam, the hen seemed like it wanted to bully the chick, so the chick got a beating despite not having a clue as to what was happening. Only the victor, the mighty old hen, ate with relish."

Mom looks around, her eyes roaming like clouds. She takes from Dad's words in his journal, makes translucent copies of his words, translating them into her own memory.

"苜蓿, alfalfa for the chickens. 白菜, napa cabbage, chopped and mixed with cornmeal, which I'd leave in a bowl on the floor. When my 老妈 (old ma) wasn't paying attention, I'd scatter 白米 (milled rice) and sunflower seeds in the grass as a treat. Insects flying toward lights at night thumped to the ground, and when they dropped, I caught them in jars and kept them until morning to feed my chickens."

My parents return from a second trip to the store with mint, peppers, and tomato starters to add to the kale and cucumber plants that 李枝 brought from her garden. Mom moves the dirt in curves, tides, and scoops. Moving within and growing out of herself, in curves, tides, scoops. Until she runs out of memory. Until memory runs out of her.

"Insect hunting around the house at night. Quail egg hunting in the field the next morning," my dad continues his memory. Silvery stem of history. "We ate all types of grass.

We chewed on their ends and sucked out the juice."

Some of the grass from the yard gets into the living room, fresh and slightly dusty.

"My chickens were orange and black and white, colourful, very tall, long legs, very clean," Mom brags. "I swept their coop daily and placed layers of fresh dry grass down while they ran about the fields. They didn't come back until nighttime. I called to them at night—*gu gu gu!* They recognized the sound of my voice. They always returned to me."

"*Gu gu gu!*" Mom calls for us, all tangy and sweet. "Time for lunch, 月月!"

"*Gu gu gu!*" And Emily puts down her book and rises from the couch.

"My hens produced eggs twice the size of our neighbours' hens, so people would come from all over to trade with us— two of their eggs for one of ours. But my 老妈 would say, one for one since they were our neighbours. We used the eggs to raise new chicks around May and June. People travelled really far to trade eggs for breeding.

"I loved my chickens. They weren't just for eggs and were my pets. I liked to memorize English terms and biology with a chicken tucked under my arm. Whenever I smiled, they pecked my teeth because I always fed them rice. They mistook my teeth for grains of rice."

Gu gu gu!

Running through the grass, running to her. Even in the

green, someone is starving. Even in the blue, there is hunger. Little 月月 jumps in a flurry of feathers into Mom's arms and starts pecking her all over her face, tasting her, eating her, splitting the difference between one face and the second, teeth like hard grains of rice, biting, soft teeth, partially crystalline granules, between one's face and the mother.

Emily and I eat out of bowls my mom left on the table for us. We're starving, even though neither of us have done much all day. Even Little 月月 shows evidence of labour, the curve of her left cheekbone smeared with dirt.

李枝 shares a story about her childhood as well while we eat, about how she and her siblings used to climb a rope down the side of a cliff to swim and catch fish in the river below.

"Chickens in the backyard!" 李枝 sighs loudly. "But the winters here are so long, so cold. They would freeze." 冻死—die off in the winter, fate of ice.

I brew ginseng tea.

"Some of the grass got into the living room," 李枝 says, sipping slowly from her cup.

李枝 leaves when her cup is empty. "The winters here," she says, leaning her weight against the banister to slip her shoes on. "You would need to invite the hens into your bed!"

Upstairs, the shower turns on and off as my parents take turns washing the dirt from their bodies. Dad lies down for a nap and encourages Mom to rest too, but she returns to the garden. I stand at the kitchen sink, cleaning the dishes, watching my mom through the small window.

She's thinner than before. Noticeably smaller, like a child, preoccupied with her task. At dusk, I call to her. There are pink and gold iridescent flecks on the skin of her neck. The marks are subtle, they stretch up to her jaw; around each of her eyes there is a sky-blue, orbital ring, and depending on the angle the light is reflecting on her, she is either intense, pale, or golden, out of focus.

"Where did you go today?" I ask her, despite knowing the answer. I'm holding an old rag in my hand, which I use to dry the counter before disposing of it in the garbage.

She holds up a jar for me to see, holds the jar oddly in her hand—she hasn't caught anything. Her hand moves like a barbule. There is even iridescence in her movements. Flat, elongated, twisting hand. I see a bed of grass in the jar. A few morning glory heads—white star in a pink cup—in a glass jar, through the prism of moonlight, moon through the prism of sun, stars through the prism of sea, see, when I cut into any fruit, *look*: nature betrays itself. Skin gives way to rind, gives way to orange teardrops, crystals, jewels. Nature is full of betrayal in this sense. A palmful of fibrous secrets offered up on a dish, in wedges, slivers, delightfully cold, pithy.

The desire to be loved is everlasting. The desire to be loved outlasts love, is last to love, and lastly, love, which begins on a pasture, on dirt floors, in the grooves of straw sandals in damp grass where the hens peck for corn kernels, at the end of a frayed rope swinging out over a yellow river, on the thin speckled shell of a quail egg.

Cracked shell, fissure, pebble split.

Love, come where light splays forth.

Love, come drawn to light.

⁂

How sweet to see her enjoying the day.

She holds up a jar, a plate, for me to see. She holds up a plate, pieces of sliced fruit, slices of an orange moon. I eat.

Cloudy relief, the table green, wedges of fruit coruscating under plastic wrap.

Gate of a factory. Lamp pole, evening time. 蝼蛄 (mole crickets) family of burrowing insects, plump, cylindrical, full, fleshy, agricultural pest. Fly and drop on the ground. Fly and drop on the ground. Evening. Catch them in a jar. The chickens are in a frenzy. Catch them mid-iridescent. Mid-transcendence. Catch them so lightly. So lightly catch the evening in a jar. Lightly, scaly, fly the hen to her nest. Lightly, singly, rewind its star of fruit, peeling memory, singing, light full of fruit.

All morning, the long morning, languid July bliss.

04

FLOATING OUT OF the rain, at their most graceful, the lights leading up to the airport terminal spread out like hyacinth bulbs, mauve, purple, and blue, and below each light, light spread by rain, delicate fountains of light pouring over tired travellers awaiting their rides, there 茄茄 stands, with a single suitcase by the open gates, holding a neck pillow in the crook of her arm, her headphones dangling around her neck. She touches her hair once before running out into the rain.

月月, the one who is six, is opening the car door, 茄茄's name already filling her mouth. 月月, the one who is twelve, is opening the trunk, pushing the jackets into a pile and throwing aside the ice scraper to make enough room for a suitcase. 茄茄 puts her things into the trunk and gets into the passenger seat. Littlest 月月 reaches around the headrest with her fingers and tickles 茄茄's neck, Little 月月 sees this and blushes fiercely, pushing her head out the window for air.

The sun is starting to rise. Rising, kneeling, on perfect, empty clouds, clearing a blueway ahead. With all of us squeezed together, the car feels snug, secretive, on the road.

"You must want to sleep," Dad says to 茄茄.

"I'm full of energy. I slept the whole flight. I only had to get up to use the toilet once." 茄茄 cranes her neck to look at us in the back seat. "Hi, 月月." She beams. "Is my English good?" She laughs. 我就会说这么一点点! (I can only speak this much!)

We drive straight home without making any stops. 茄茄 has her phone out the entire time filming the road. It's hot and dry, and when we get home, the grass on our lawn feels tough, brittle. Mom and Emily hurry down from the porch when they see us, and Dad has to shoo them from the driveway in order to park the car.

"Let me see you." Mom spins 茄茄 around. 你怎么还没有我高? (How come you haven't reached my height yet?) "I remember you were so much taller than 月月."

"She's older than 月月! When they're kids, a few years makes a big difference," Dad says and carries 茄茄's suitcase into the house. He suggests we continue our conversation indoors. It's still early and a weekend morning.

"I brought you all something. I know you said not to—it's just a small thing, just some snacks for Emily and 月月. You can't buy them here." 我知道在这很难买到好吃的 (I know it's hard to get good food here).

"There's no rush." Mom motions for Emily to bring 茄茄 a chair. "Sit, sit. You want water? I'll pour you water. I made breakfast." 吃点 (Eat a little). "Of course you brought us gifts. How is your dad? He told me his business is struggling."

"You said it yourself, eh? There's no rush, so why talk about that now?" Dad pours himself a bowl of cereal and offers some to 茄茄, who smiles, shakes her head, and laughs.

"Can I look at your backyard?" 茄茄 unlocks her suitcase and pulls out a plastic bag full of treats. She puts the bag on the table and gives Emily an encouraging wink. Next, she takes out a stack of clothes for my parents, which she leaves on the floor by her suitcase. My mom waits for her on the other side of the sliding glass door. 茄茄 stands to go join her. On the way over, to my surprise, she leans close to my ear and says, 你还是跟以前一样，月月.

"月月, you are the same as before."

They're gone.

I don't know when they left, but they're gone: Littlest 月月 and Little 月月.

They woke up early this morning to go to the airport to pick up 茄茄. They both showered. They looked prim and proper sitting in the car. When we were parked in the pick-up area, waiting, Little 月月 said, *I can't think of anything to say.* "But no one's even said anything yet," I said. They were a little shy when 茄茄 first appeared, but overall, they were quiet in a happy way. Littlest 月月 even massaged 茄茄's shoulders through the gap between the back of the seat and the head-rest. Of all of us, she was the closest to 茄茄 and naturally most excited. Little 月月 was colder but only because she could not sleep all night in anticipation. There was strength in her hand that grabbed my arm. Where is that hand now? Is it in the garden, stroking the back of a green leaf? Is it on the grass, parsing the clovers for double growth? Where is Littlest 月月 and Little 月月, and what did 茄茄 mean by that—你还是跟以前一样?

I don't recognize 茄茄 at all. She looks completely different. The voice mingling with my mom's voice out in the backyard is radiant, clinging, nothing like the hoarse, girlish voice that once called to me through the thick haze of chirping crickets.

"Did you hear the rain?"

"It rained? That's why the grass is wet then."

"茄茄." I bring myself to my full height and call to my cousin. "茄茄, do you want to go somewhere with me?"

I explain that there is a trail I want to bring 茄茄 to. There are only two bikes, so Emily won't be able to come with us.

The tomato plant has grown so tall in a month that its leaves reach through the wire and brush at 茄茄's knees. She's wearing a billowy long-sleeved top over wide-leg pants. Her clothes are wrinkled from the long flight.

"I won't be able to sleep tonight if I don't tire myself out somehow," 茄茄 says.

"Would you like to get changed first?" I ask.

"I may take a shower after we get back," 茄茄 says, leaning forward to smell the leaf in my mom's hand. "Say, 月月, do you still like singing in the bath?"

"You really won't overheat?" I look at the bowed figures of 茄茄 and my mom. "I can lend you some of my clothes if you don't have anything. I'm going to apply sunscreen."

"I'll come with you." 茄茄 claps her hands. "You didn't know that? You liked singing in the bath. Everyone has heard your singing."

The dark circles beneath 茄茄's eyes disappear when she looks up at the light. She applies sunscreen to her face, her neck, her hands, and her ankles. Even the skin between her fingers, she rubs with sunscreen, lacing her fingers together and lathering: hands, fingers, fingertips, wrists.

"Shall we go? You can take Emily's bike."

"It's been a long time since I last rode a bike."

"You will remember," I reassure her.

A morning-like mist is pressing into the house through the windows.

Everyone, she says. Everyone has heard my singing.

茄茄's body will remember how to ride a bike even if she doesn't. Touch can bring back memory—memory of touch—touches memory—memory touches—lighter with each touch—until memory has no weight—layers—suspense—hearing—a morning-like mist presses in—mind in open memory—clearest window—silver morning—cattails wave on the road, tiny islands of wild sage—waving, wavering, light with loss, silver with pride.

Silver, reflective, repetitious.

Silver wheels, spokes, speaking, speech. The bike speeches across the pavement. The bike spoke silvering, steel. Beneath the tires pebbles spring up, rocks fly up, threatening to cut our ankles. Grey threat, sharp floor-wind. I am squinting and 茄茄 is squinting. *Look*, I remove one hand from the handlebar to point—yellow nutsedge, chipmunk, spring peeper hiding in the shade, a garden snake squirming on its back, white belly exposed. The palms of my hands are sticky from the rubber grips and covered in grime.

Grasshoppers evade our wheels at the last possible second, opening their wings and revealing moth faces on their backs. 茄茄 squeals and ducks her head.

Both bikes are on the small side because my parents purchased them second-hand from yard sales for Emily and me. We ride fast, though somewhat awkwardly, up the trail into the woods.

"What time is it?" 茄茄 calls breathlessly from behind.

"It's almost three o'clock."

"No way! It's three in the morning for me then."

茄茄 stops her bike in the middle of the trail for a water break. Light forays through overlapping foliage, almond-slices of light, green and yellow ovals, nacreous. An elegant gathering of surfaces, inlets of light.

"People will soon be driving north to see the autumn leaves."

Just as I say this, a leaf falls from above and lands by the front wheel of my bike.

"Will you sleep well tonight?"

茄茄 doesn't answer at first, then she's laughing, laughing, pulling her shirt forward and letting the breeze touch her skin.

"My head is starting to hurt."

I nod. "There's a place I want to show you a little up ahead, but we don't need to go today."

"What is it? What do you want to show me? I have no idea how I managed to get this far."

"It's not really anything. If we continue on this path, we'll reach a stream. We might see more animals if we go this way."

茄茄 is already turning her bike around.

"Do you remember when I took Shushu's bike and you sat on the back? It was such a bumpy ride, and the bike was too big, even with the both of us on it."

Shushu; shūshu; 叔叔; uncle; a child's form of address for any young man; anyone, everyone, *everyone has heard your singing.*

I used to sing for my family. My uncle, aunt, grandma, grandpa, and parents, sitting together in a well-lit room. 茄茄 snuck up behind me and made bunny ears with her fingers. "Keep going!" My family would say each time I stopped singing to chase 茄茄.

茄茄 pedals, one small kick at a time.

I want her to keep going.

✿

茄茄 keeps commenting on the 空间 (spaciousness) of our neighbourhood, how 矮 (short) and 平 (flat) the houses are, how 可爱 (cute). We're taking a stroll together to show her around the area. She's walking up ahead with my mom, chatting about massage therapy, acupuncture, menstrual pains. Emily and I walk behind them, listening in on their conversation somewhat. My dad is farther down the street with his camera, ordering us to stop every so often so he can take our photo.

We walk behind the houses, where the trees are, and come to the bridge. The rusted arch of the bridge falls gracefully across a running stream; butterflies chase themselves into their rippling reflections, petals answering a mirror.

"This evening," 茄茄 says to me with a mischievous grin, "shall we go into the city, just you and me?"

茄茄 told me her job involves connecting buyers to suppliers. She told me a lot more about what she does, but I couldn't understand much of it. I just know she studied business.

茄茄 has been sleeping in Emily's bedroom. It's an easy arrangement, as Emily has continued to sleep on the floor of my room. 茄茄's been talking about wanting to go into the city before she leaves to do some shopping and sightseeing, experience the nightlife—看夜景, as she puts it, view the night scene.

"The last train is at eleven and the buses in this neighbourhood don't run past ten."

茄茄's face is still there, leaning attentively forward.

"Does everyone drive?"

"I can't afford to."

Steam rises up from the water. Autumnal shadow, fall's quivering pulse.

"But I just graduated," I blurt before 茄茄 can turn away. "I'll get a job and move to the city, so the next time you come, you can stay with me."

"If only my English were better."

"I'm serious. Stay with me next time you come. I'll show you around the city."

"I'll come. Sure, I'll come." 茄茄 raises herself on her toes to pat my head. "All right, I'll come stay with you. I'll hold you to it, so you'd better keep your promise. You'd better not forget."

茄茄 stands so close to me and is always touching my head without permission.

Drops of rain—液晶, drops of sudden rain. 茄茄 is viewing the rain, so is my mom, so are Emily and my dad. They are standing in the rain on the bridge, viewing the sky, the stream is breaking, they are running in the direction of the house while laughing. Who is laughing? Laughing brokenly. Crystals are falling. Memory crystallizes and falls. The rain is calling us home.

"I experienced something unusual on my flight," 茄茄 tells us. "The woman seated next to me was crying. She told me she was on her way to a funeral, though she didn't say how she was related to the deceased person, and I didn't want to pry. Whenever the flight attendants came by with drinks or snacks, she would fold her napkin twice, dab at her cheeks, and turn to me—she had the aisle seat—she'd turn to me and smile genuinely and offer me her share of food. She even let me have her blanket. She had such a polite way of mourning."

Our house has flattened and turned to water. Every house on our street has turned to water. The street lamps turned to trees. There is a pond in the spot where each house had stood. I can see around the street's crescent; sight blossoms freely with each gust of wind.

Water accumulates at our feet, rippling like clay on a throwing wheel, each ripple restoring the previous wave so that nothing spills over. We are in the woods together, and if it is raining, then it is the sunny kind, the sprinkling, glittering kind. When I am next to my family like this, I feel as if I can remember my entire life, my dreams laid before me like a silk blanket; I feel as if nothing is lost and I will never lose anything.

茄茄 uncurls her fist and reveals a flat stone. Emily takes

the stone from 茄茄 and walks toward the pond. She tells us she can skip the stone ten times. On the surface of the water, a string of dimples; the breaking point never appears.

Time stands still in a mother's heart: the only place you never age. Time is still in my heart. I can let everything come into focus at that core.

Emily tosses another stone into the air and it lands perfectly in my pocket.

05

IN THE END, Mom says something about her health to 茄茄 after all. I spy from the staircase as 茄茄 listens to my mom, nodding stiffly, then wrapping her arm around Mom's shoulders. The knowledge that my mom is finally revealing her condition to someone else in our family gives me some ease. She talks so quietly, I can hear my footsteps on the carpeted steps.

茄茄 watches as I step past them to pick up the guitar from the corner of the room. I join them on the couch, playing what chords I know. Sitting between 茄茄 and me, Mom begins to hum, her shoulders gently shaking.

Several weeks after 茄茄 leaves, Mom stops tending her garden. She splays herself over the kitchen table with her head resting on her forearm and won't say a word to anyone. She'll only raise her head, tilting her ear, red from where it was pressed against her arm, when she hears my dad's singing from upstairs. Dad has been singing. He seems to be living in the past, singing all his favourite songs from his student days. He gives the impression that he's doing it for Mom, but there is a feeling of going away in his voice. An unpredictable, frivolous blue. A familiar tune—passed between him and only him.

recognition 认 repetition 重 response 应
rèn   chóng   yìng

Echo, reaction, fold, duplicate, over and over, reverberate, overlap, superpose, pile up, recite, stay behind, recapitulate, pass from mouth to mouth.

Echo, fold, duplicate, stay. Pass from mouth to mouth.

I feel everything in my usual blue manner. I have not forgotten about my dad's health—we have known for some time that he has high blood pressure, but it wasn't until I sat next to him during a doctor's visit that the details came to me, all at once, words whistling through narrow leaves. He said he lost his balance twice and laughed shakily. The details came to me like bamboo. His hands were shaking. Twice, he lost his balance. He shook. The movements happened twice.

Still, on the drive back, I started a fight with him. Laboured breathing filled the car as my dad's chest rattled. I experienced my first hailstorm from the inside of a car, my dad in the driver's seat next to me. Small white pebbles struck the roof of the car and scattered down the sides, the sound of the ice as pleasant as it was terrible. Our car became a tunnel, a cocoon. We were dark with memory. I wanted to be trapped with my dad forever, ice-proof, but he said, "Mom is waiting for you at home." When I looked at him again from the passenger seat, the hailstorm was inside, it was coming from me.

"I'm sorry," I said.

I thought my dad would be angry with me.

"I'm sorry," I repeated myself. "I know you have high blood pressure, and I still make you angry."

"Nobody's perfect," my dad said. "We can only try. I have to try too."

It was the closest I came to receiving an apology from my dad, and after an argument that was entirely my doing. "I'm sorry," I said. My heart was looped with guilt.

"Don't let your mom see you crying," he said. "Her health," he said. "We shouldn't make her worry."

Our car was parked and my dad was getting ready to unlock the front door.

"I love you," I said.

He stood still on the porch for a moment and let me wrap my arms around him.

Echo, reaction, fold, duplicate.

Over and over, reverberate.

My dad is singing. I pressed my head against his chest, trapped his voice in me, his voice like a bird's that I hear in my ear in the garden, his voice that swoops overhead and strikes its shadow against the roof.

✲✲

I leave my slippers neatly by the sliding glass door and change into my mom's gardening shoes. I cut stems of kale, cut basil above the leaf buds, cut sage and thyme, pick peppers and tomatoes. Field mice scurry behind the wooden planks by the fence. Soft shape of rabbits in soft darkness.

Our smoke tree has changed colour—mauve stems and orange plumage. I didn't know this could happen. My hands are frothy, my veins running in a hundred streams. My hands are clustered, sometimes yellow, translucent, in the rain.

I never thought I'd swim out of memory and find it ahead of me.

"Can I hug you?" I ask my mom, who does not move in bed.

I wrap her blankets around her and draw her curtains but not all the way, the room slightly dusty with light.

Emily spends hours by Mom's pillow, whispering into her ear. Whichever way Mom is lying in bed, Emily will take on that position: on her back, on her side, on her side with her knees brought up to her chest, on her stomach. Then, smiling sadly, she glides down the hallway to her room. I call to her, gently lifting the silver thread between us.

"What?" Emily's answer is tart.

"Will you help me with the garden?"

"Isn't it too early, though? If you water the plants while the sun is this high ..."

"I'm thinking of planting some flowers. I need your help digging a hole."

"It's almost winter."

"Then it's almost spring."

Quite without warning, Emily raises her head and shoulders from the pillow. "I can't be lying here. I have to study."

"Emily ..."

"You don't need to worry about the garden. Mom is planning to add another section next spring. We'll cut everything before it gets too cold and save the roots." Emily raises herself to a sitting position and adds absent-mindedly, "You didn't know?"

She seems to be in no great hurry to study.

The first chill of the season is beginning to creep up from the floorboards. Moths will occasionally find their way into the house and build their nests within the light fixtures. While I've been pampering myself with my sad little dream world, Emily has already made spring plans with our mom.

Joining Emily on her bed, I place my arm across her shoulders as I saw 茄茄 do for Mom. I expect her to cock an eyebrow at me in wonder before shoving me off, but the shape in my arms feels subdued, lonely.

Sunlight thaws the window. The windows are made from warmth, from gold; the window frames are made from silver. Moths melt into the warm light. Silver moths, spun from my dreams. Over and over again, reverberate, spun from mouth to mouth, this fine thread between us.

"Did I ever apologize to you for burning your wrist?"

"No, you didn't."

"Oh? Well, I'm sorry."

"It's okay."

"I'm sorry, Emily, for burning your wrist."

"It's okay. I forgive you."

"I'm sorry."

Emily was spun from snow in a fish's mouth. My sister the peach that Mom plucked from a winter tree.

My sister the fish wish, the peach womb.

"You don't need to forgive me just because I'm your sister," I say.

"I see."

"Emily?"

"But I can't do anything for her."

"You know that's not true."

"Why didn't she tell Wàipó sooner? She thinks there is nothing she can do for Grandma. Just like how there is nothing I can do for her."

"Isn't that wrong, though? Don't we only need to do the dishes once or twice and tend to the garden when she can't?"

"Yeah, you're right."

"We can both do a lot for her."

Emily sits up straight and fixes her hair.

"I am going to study now, I'm serious. I have to study if I want to get a good job."

"Well, good luck."

But she does not leave the room. She sits on the bed, repeatedly jabbing the carpet with her toe. Framed by the window, Emily's outline is silver, thready.

"Do you miss her?"

"Who do you mean? 茄茄?"

Emily lifts the end of the curtain and drapes it over her face.

"Well?" she asks, lips moving beneath the white fabric. "Do you?"

"These curtains have never been washed. Of course I miss her. Do you have to ask? But I've lived my entire life without her."

"*I* miss her. I finished all the snacks she brought."

"I miss her too! If I think about what kind of missing that is, or try to figure out who exactly I miss—my memory of her, or this new her I'm still getting to know ... There's a difference. I'm numb, I can't remember why I'm sad, and the sadness doesn't go away."

"Don't think so hard."

"Thinking is remembering!"

While I was busy talking, Emily had taken the curtain off her face to stare out the window.

"It's snowing—look!"

I squeeze to her side.

"It's snowing!"

"Māma, it's snowing!"

I hear the curtains drawn in the other room and my parents' excited voices. As I lean against the window, catching the first sight of snow, I think about how likely it is we'll all go to the lake together, to see the water in winter inlaid with silver.

Maybe 茄茄 will be there too.

part 05

EMILY ROTATES THE CERAMIC Dalmatian by its base in order to admire it from every angle. "It's so glossy." Her voice has a hint of jealousy.

"It's for you," I say.

"Don't you want to keep it?" She looks at me warmly while stroking the dog's floppy ears. There is a deliberate pace to her strokes. There is vulnerability, a certain measure of attention paid to each caress, hesitation, as well as something in her eyes that tells me she wants my opinion on something. "What should I play?" she asks.

"What should you play?" I return the question, confused.

Emily continues to strum the instrument in her palm.

Our living room begins to fill rapidly with shadow and light. The asymmetries of the room become exaggerated: one second the room is stretched long, endless yet two dimensional, another second it is short again, compact. To my eye, the entire house is spinning. I hurry to the sliding glass door, reaching with both arms to draw the curtains on either side, but light insists; light presses through the dark cloth. My shadow extends from my body like a sister body; I stretch my palms to my face and a second set of fingers spread over my eyes.

"What do you want me to play?" Johnny asks, holding the neck of his banjo with one hand, strumming with the other.

"Come," Johnny says. "Why are you hiding? I have something I want to show you."

I peek out from behind ten shadow fingers, ten fingers of light. Johnny's outline overlaps the arms of our couch. The strings of his banjo shine forth brightly, making me squint. I notice a trembling beneath Johnny's fingers. A delicious swelling.

Johnny takes my hand and pulls me into his lap, raises his banjo over our heads and lowers it in front of me. My hand is still in his. Johnny takes my fingers and presses them onto the strings. Bits of coloured light fall through the kitchen window.

"You sing—do you?" Johnny asks.

Johnny's hair is wet. I didn't notice until now. Water drips off the tips onto my neck, making me shiver. He clings to me, fanning my ear with his breath.

The room has become the inside of a cocoon. Water drips off the tipped centres of my pupils. Icicles of piercing light.

"I was waiting for you." I can barely speak above a whisper. "I was waiting for you to come back, and you never came."

I have reached memory's limits. Instead, music pleads forth from me; pale green notes tremble out from me, floating, fawning, silver lines stretching to the ceiling, silk web drifting over us.

I imagine Johnny waiting beneath a street lamp outside the university gates with a book out, his bag slung across his chest, a delicate wool scarf wrapped around his neck. He raises two fingers from the page to motion to me, pressing his chin down on his scarf. I hurry across the street to him, into his arms.

I imagine arriving in his arms, landing into him, wings clipped by snow. He'll remove the glove from my hand and raise my shivering palm to his lips. It's so easy to imagine.

My first impression of Johnny across our classroom was that he seemed always to be on the verge of saying something ugly—I imagine feeling Johnny's breath like a bright shadow against the palm of my hand. He'll take my hand and I'll slip my fingers between his fingers, packing my fingers onto his fingers. We'll go, layer by layer, deeper and deeper, into the snow, and he'll say, "Watch out for the puddles," and pull me close. His voice soft like mountain darkness; his words always like a story about to begin.

"What are you thinking about?" I ask him. His outline has become more obscure. He's fading, and quickly, but still I can see the inscrutable smile on his face.

His answer: "The past."

I know this will all go to pieces.

"You okay?" Emily's voice rises to the foreground like bells jingling down sand dunes. I can't help myself from reaching out and touching her face. The skin on her cheek swells when I touch it—she's smiling, telling me Mom's in the backyard. "Do you want to come with me?" she's asking. "Let's go show Mom the ceramic dog together," she's saying.

"Mom will love it," Emily says. "She might try to keep it for herself."

"Dalmatians are Mom's favourite type of dog," she says.

⁂

小马过河 (xiǎo mǎ guò hé)—"The Little Horse Crosses the River"—is a children's story every child in China hears in elementary school about a little horse that learns to be independent.

One day, the little horse is tasked by his mother to bring a bag of wheat to the mill, but along the way, the little horse is blocked by a river. The little horse sees an old bull grazing by the side of the river, so he runs to the bull and asks, "Can you tell me whether I can cross this river?"

The bull replies, "The river is shallow and only rises to the calf. You will be able to cross."

The little horse thanks the bull and hurries to cross, but

just then a squirrel jumps in his way, shouting, "Little horse! Don't cross! You will drown if you try to cross this river."

In my mom's version of the story, the squirrel even says something about the river taking the life of his cousin, Little Red. "Xiǎo Hóng! Xiǎo Hóng!"

Hearing the squirrel, the little horse is unwilling to cross the river. After much dread and trepidation, he eventually does attempt to cross the river and finds that the water is neither as shallow as the bull described nor as deep and injurious as in the squirrel's account.

"Can't horses swim?" I asked my mom the first time I heard the tale.

"What is the moral of the story?" she asked me.

"Squirrels are stupid."

"Be serious."

"Squirrels are stupid. Horses are stupid."

"The moral is that you have to try things for yourself. You have to decide."

⁎⁎⁎

I received a call from someone I had forgotten about. From M. She said her name was Mary, and it took me a moment to remember that we'd met.

It took me a moment. It took some time, but eventually, I called her back.

O2

I STOOD UP and brushed the dirt from my knees and went back in from the balcony. The apartment we were in was identical to ours in size and layout, every unit copy-paste stacked on top of one another for nine floors, but this apartment was a lot cleaner than ours, sparser too, everything from the furniture to the decor sensibly considered and methodically arranged. A chestnut display case stood next to the piano; on the top shelf sat a mini bonsai tree in a low ceramic bowl, and on the wall behind the bonsai was a watercolour painting in a frame. Tall stools were lined up against the window, giving the living room the feel of an outdoor noodle shop.

My mom was sitting on one of the stools, speaking to the woman who lived in the apartment. The woman was telling my mom how you didn't need to be a "real Catholic" to enroll in the nearby Catholic school, which was more prestigious and "better for the kids" than the public school that Emily and I attended. When I interrupted, the woman smiled at me and gave me a piece of guava candy from her purse. I unwrapped the candy and held it up to the sun, green like a dragonfly's head, intense with light. My mom would sigh occasionally and drag her nails through the cracks on the wooden sill, and say something about being a "bad mom." During lapses in conversation, both women stared forlornly at us children, sometimes without recognition.

I went out again onto the balcony, my tongue wrapped around the guava candy, cheeks sucked in. I rolled the candy to one side of my mouth and asked the girl crouching next to Emily where she got the eggs from.

The girl was a year older than Emily and had recently moved into our building. She was born here and didn't speak any Mandarin. I had only spoken to her for the first time that day. We bumped into her and her mom in the lobby of our apartment building, and they had invited us up with the promise of showing us some turtle eggs.

"We found them," the girl answered me over her knees. Her Coke-bottle glasses made her look skeptical of her own reply.

She was afraid that I was going to accuse her of stealing the eggs from the mother turtle, thus, wishing to establish trust, she offered to let me hold the eggs, to *touch* them if I wanted. The balcony was a hunk of concrete framed by rusted poles.

In the middle, in front of us, was the cardboard box, stood vertically, filled with silver sand. I wanted to touch the eggs very much. I got down on my knees and stretched out my hand. The sand shifted, sprinkled, sang little *sssshh*s, and the eggs were there, exposed, their sleeping faces bright and pale. I picked one up in my sand-powdered palm; it felt like a delicate pouch in my hand, white membrane like thinly diffused starlight. I imagined a pulse like a tear trickling down my cheek.

"You'll bring the turtles back when they hatch?" I asked.

"Yes, yes." The girl's mom was talking from inside the apartment. There was hesitation in her answer.

I felt bad and thankful at the same time. I went home, leaving my mom and sister behind, taking the stairs down two flights to our unit. My dad was making dinner when I came in. I shared the sink with him, washing my hands under a gush of warm water. The skin on my hands felt leathery, too soft. When I placed my hands under the water they bloated and filled with air.

"Call your mom to dinner," my dad said to me.

"That place gives me an eerie feeling."

"You're not taking the stairs alone, are you?"

"How come we don't have any Chinese art on our walls?"

"Don't we put your drawings on the fridge?"

"Ha! You're funny."

"Go on and call your mom to dinner. And don't take the stairs alone."

In the bachelor building, the apartments were all one-bedroom but had an area that was meant to be an extension of the living room that could be used as a den. My parents had installed a curtain between the living room and den and turned that space into their bedroom so that Emily and I could take the main bedroom. The woman upstairs shared her room with her daughter and used their den as a home library, which I was incredibly jealous of—my family didn't own any bookshelves.

"Shūjià? Bookshelf?" My dad emphasized the proper tonal marks, correcting my clumsy Mandarin. "Shǔjià, that's summer vacation. And shūjiā, that's calligrapher or calligraphist. Shūjiā is a loser, as in, someone who loses a gambling game, as opposed to the yíngjiā, winner." He softened his expression and touched the back of my head. "We just go to the library. Okay?"

But I could not express to him then how I didn't want to own books. What I wanted was to organize the books I read in neat, colour-shifting rows, even if at the end of the month I had to chuck them all in a bag and return them to the library. My tongue rose and fell, dotted and slashed, a stumble of excess vowels. Nothing like my dad's clean strokes.

I had wanted to touch the turtle eggs too. Even though I knew better. Even though they weren't for people to just decide to pick up for a moment because they felt like it. I felt terribly guilty. I trembled with gratitude.

Emily's hands were grey from touching the sand in the turtle box. She waved goodbye to the woman and her daughter with her little grey hand and ran after me down the stairs. Mom didn't come home until a half hour later, when the rest of us had already finished eating.

"You should see how they organized their space." Mom picked at the food in her bowl.

"She's divorced with one child, isn't she?" Dad asked.

"Right, right," Mom spoke nervously.

That morning we had moved our car from its spot in the underground garage to a parking space outside the apartment. I could tell that the move dispirited my parents. They worried that the car would be quick to wear down under the sun and rain, but we could no longer afford to park it in the garage.

I preferred the outdoor parking lot to the underground garage. There were lilac shrubs growing over the painted white lines, fragrant petals drifting city-blue and periwinkle, and a cherry tree, short and twisted, next to the splintered fence surrounding the basketball court. Dad would take our photos on the patchy grass, and if a basketball bounced out of bounds, the boys playing there would ask him to throw it back. I felt my love for him strongly, watching him bend to pick up the basketball, then lift his arms over his head. I felt love for the boys, who trusted he would throw back their ball. Standing around in their oversized tanks, sweat dripping patiently down their backs. The ball would *deng* on the ground once, smushing some weeds, *deng-deng-deng*, then the shouting would start back up, the sound of pushing and slapping, and laughter, and my dad's camera shutter, going off with a click, wind tipping the leaves.

Since there was nothing to do in our cramped apartment, we would often go outside and spend hours at the park. "This is free to enjoy!" My dad would say between camera shutters. "You can come to the park for free and look at any tree!"

I was staring out the window one night, abstruse shapes of construction blocking the sky, machine arms like giant mantises crooning between the pines, when I saw two orbs swimming in moonlight. Two orbs circling each other like distant fish. I threw my face into my pillow, then jumped back up to the window and began to blink. I didn't know what I was seeing: perhaps helicopter searchlights were shining through peach mist, some private reflection of lightning. I jumped to the window and began to blink. How fortunate to be alive and not understand!

⁎⁎

Before placing the turtle egg back into the sand, I thought to myself, *Remember, remember.*

I put my hands under the warm water gushing. *Remember, remember.*

One intersection down from our apartment building was the condo where most of my elementary school classmates lived. Many of the students lived either in houses next to the school or in the condo, and then a few of us lived in the red-brick apartment building. On Halloween night, we would gather from all over the neighbourhood in the lobby of the condo, because the condo handed out bags of candy to every child. You had to live in the condo to partake in the lobby trick-or-treat, but no one ever checked.

Emily and I would follow tenants from their cars to the main entrance, wait for them to scan their key cards, then slip past them. Security guards often came by with mild threats, and I'd tell them I was waiting for my parents, I was waiting for my friend—there was nothing they could do.

We got used to waiting in the condo lobby, sometimes spending an hour or two there after school just waiting for our parents to come back from work. Emily beelined to the fish tank every time, a massive 150-gallon ensemble of glass canopies and polyresin caves. She pressed her forehead right up against the glass, breath fogging up the view each time she opened her mouth in wonder.

It was the carpet that absorbed my attention, my foot-steps. I cushioned into it, soft and red and clean, it stretched throughout the entirety of the lobby. I would just stand there, staring down at my feet while Emily zipped around me. There was also a swimming pool I could see past the fish tank that was always unoccupied.

I knew this girl from my grade who lived in the condo at the time. Her name was Rebecca. We weren't in the same homeroom, so we hardly ever spoke. She was getting mail from the lobby one afternoon and saw me there with Emily. She had waved to me from behind an artificial ficus tree; her short legs and tough knees looked intertwined with the stunted branches shooting from the pot. We saw each other a few more times after that, each of us waving shyly to the other, until finally she approached me at school and invited me over to her place. I had always wondered what the condo units looked like, whether the nice plush lobby carpet stretched across the hall on every floor, so I agreed right away. We decided I would go over to her place after school the very same day.

Rebecca lived on the sixth floor, same as us, but our windows were different. The trees from her winter window looked like sticks of incense. The people moving below like the last wisps of smoke. I got down from the sill, feeling dizzy.

Rebecca opened the freezer and passed me a Drumstick, not a mini but a whole, full-sized, choco-dipped vanilla scoop on a wafer cone. When I expressed worry about not being able to finish my ice cream, she shrugged and told me I could toss whatever was left, which I took as a non-answer and I sat there licking hard. It felt wasteful, forcing myself to eat the entire thing when I didn't want any more instead of getting to split it with Emily.

Rebecca passed me the ice cream from the kitchen hole. She said that's what the gap in the wall between the kitchen and the living room was called.

There were two bedrooms in addition to the living room and kitchen. It excited me that someone my age could have a whole private bedroom of their own, and so I kept opening and closing Rebecca's door until she brought me into her room and locked the door to keep me still.

Rebecca was Asian too; her family was from Taiwan. And like my family, they didn't have any Asian stuff on their walls or any Asian-style decorations, apart from one handheld fan. I decided the woman and her daughter who lived in the apartment above my family were collectors, or they were just really efficient at moving their furniture across countries and didn't have to part with anything valuable.

"Let's go to your place," Rebecca said.

She had finished explaining the backstory and significance of every plushie strewn across her bed and was moving on to the knick-knacks on her desk.

It dawned on me that Rebecca thought we lived in the same condo building.

I wanted to sit on Rebecca's bed while she painted my nails with a tiny brush, watch her slide a disk into the CD player and push "play"; I wanted her to tell me more about the sparkly statuettes her parents brought back from Paris; I wanted to go downstairs and play in the condo's tenants-only playground without having to sneak in through a hole in the fence, shimmying on my belly and clawing with my fingers like a raccoon; I wanted to get up and go to the window again, and look down at the street again, even if it scared me.

My dad had to leave work early that day because I never showed up outside Emily's classroom to pick her up. He left as early as he could, but Emily still had to wait a long time, and the teacher who stayed behind with her had to wait a long time. When I came home, my dad would not even look at me, and my mom said, "How can you be so selfish?" And as I stood there in our hallway, I remembered how on the sixth floor of the condo, the carpet was as thin as ours.

※

My family took walks in the park every night after dinner. Soon, we had many friends in the neighbourhood. I would bring my bike, which my dad had bought for ten dollars at a yard sale, the purple paint job flaking fast, revealing the bike's silver bones, and Emily would run after the blur of me, both of us flashing teeth as we whirled. I biked circles around my parents, who could liáo tiān for hours with our Asian neighbours. The people they met at the park started coming by our apartment, exchanging their shoes at the door for slippers, always bringing fruits when they came to visit—apples, pears, persimmons. Mom liked to peel mandarin oranges while she listened to gossip, leaving coiled ribbons everywhere her fingers danced.

There was a baseball diamond and a soccer field at our park, and there would often be games happening on both sides at once, so the nights were always lively. Emily and I would stand behind the bleachers and watch the soccer game, then sprint across the path to the bleachers by the baseball diamond—whichever side was cheering loudest, we would go there. We swung freely back and forth in the luminous heat of the stadium lights. All the kid athletes were white, even though our neighbourhood wasn't. I remember that detail clearly because it felt like we were intruding on their games, because they always pretended not to see us there, even though it was our park.

When the games became more frequent, a budget was approved to raise a fence around the bleachers on both sides, and the grass on the soccer field was replaced by a neon synthetic patch. I flipped over the fence by stepping along the edge of the concrete step, then climbing up onto the garbage bins. At night, once all the balls had been loaded into duffle bags and thrown into the trunks of cars, I would lie on my back on the fake grass and stare up at the sky, light orbiting my pupils.

I didn't see much of the girl from the apartment upstairs once the school year began, since she was younger than me and Catholic. But I heard from my mom that she brought the turtles back to the park. The turtles were returned to their mother and lived happily in the creek, where no one disturbed them and daffodils grew.

Rebecca and I continued to be friends, but she never did come to visit my place. I don't think her parents wanted her at the apartment complex.

03

EMILY WATCHES THE train arrive from the edge of the platform. Light splits over the back of the train like frets on a string instrument, framing us in ornamental morningness. Both of us want window seats, so we sit facing each other, shoes touching. Beyond the platform, over the metal roof of the station, we can see buses and commuter cars arriving down the hill leading from the highway. It's the rainy season between winter and spring, and in the soaked fields surrounding the tracks, there are deer grazing, scuts like cattail fluff.

"I'm excited to go downtown with you," Emily lifts her headphones to say to me.

The train is unusually quiet for a weekday morning. My reflection trembles upon the glass—the rain is coming down harder, yet somehow it is radiant on the inside, the overhead lights lending a new life to the dingy canvas seats. I nudge

Emily's foot with mine when the train passes the lake and watch her reaction from the corner of my eye.

"It's supposed to stop in the next hour," Emily says and glances around the cabin.

"Maybe I want to get wet."

Emily rests her head against the window. "Good day for the plants," she says. She closes her eyes and within a few moments has drifted off.

Mom is tending her garden again. There are now three stalks of kale growing in the raised box, tomatoes, two types of peppers, green onions, and Brussels sprouts. Long vines of a pumpkin plant cascade down the side of the fence where the backyard receives the most sun. Around the deck, she has placed small planters growing a variety of herbs. She switched to another department at her job, where the workload is lighter and doesn't require her to stand for hours. The lift in her spirits is a relief to all of us, especially Dad, who has started taking photos again, most of which are of Mom.

When we arrive at our station, Emily strides down from the steps of the train and begins walking in the opposite direction to where we're meant to go. I wait for her at the end of the platform, watching with amusement. She stays close to my side after that.

The rain stopped like she said it would. The city feels friendly and brand new. Emily swivels her head and takes her phone out for photos every few steps, a pretty smile dancing on her lively face. She seems more like a tourist than someone who was born in this city.

Emily wants to have lunch in Chinatown—it occurs to me that while Chinatown is steps away from my campus, and I've often passed through it, I've never stopped for lunch there or taken a leisurely stroll past the various shops and restaurants.

I disliked Chinatown when I was younger—spinner displays stocked with national flags and postcards lining the sidewalk, grocery stores open to the street displaying piles of odd fruit, electric signs with dull backlighting, dumpling restaurants and twenty-four-hour dim sum, racks of plain T-shirts and neon posters, loud throngs of people making their way through the shop stands, workers wearing slick rubber gloves pushing trolleys of limp vegetables, too many sounds, fragments of a language I struggled to pick up, bits of words, phrases, colours, smells.

When I started university, everyone around me spoke of Chinatown nostalgically. Everyone—not just the Asian students—longed for the eggy scent of bubble waffles, the golden batter poured into an iron griddle before being stuffed in a paper bag or cone. I couldn't relate to them at all. I felt jealous and shut out. After lectures, I would see groups of students walking over to Chinatown while I rushed to the station. I barely had enough money to cover my commute from month to month.

"You're lucky you get to have boba whenever you want,"

Emily says while pulling open the door to a tea shop. She has to use both hands to drag the door over the thick mat jammed between the frame and the floor.

Earlier, we overheard some international students saying they could go for "boba." Emily tried out the word for herself: boba, boba, boba, boba, bubble tea, bubble tea, bubble tea, boba, bubble tea. I order my drink without tapioca, and Emily can barely look at me after that. There isn't anywhere to sit inside. I pay for our drinks and we step back onto the sidewalk. We stand on the street in the light, sipping through thick, colourful straws. Light magnifies around us. Light reveals itself to be many unique flowers, around Emily, around me, continually revived by each cloud burst, silvery, transparent flowers of light.

"The first time I tried bubble tea was the year we went back to China," I tell Emily. "Jiā Jiā took me out with her friends. I had trouble ordering. All the drinks on the menu looked overwhelming."

I lead Emily down a flight of cracked steps into a variety store, stopping on the way to toss my empty cup in a bin. The store manager acknowledges us with an absent-minded wave of her hand, her other hand holding a phone to her ear. I can't recognize the dialect she speaks and have trouble understanding her. I explore the aisles eagerly, asking Emily if we need a new teapot, or a bamboo toothbrush, how about an earpick? A back scratcher? We decide on a ceramic bowl, which the manager charges seven dollars for and helps us wrap in a sheet of newspaper.

"She's scamming us," Emily declares in Mandarin, which the store manager pretends not to hear, humming while she punches buttons on the register.

We go into a grocery store next, looping around the frozen food aisles, gawking at the giant pink squid and feeling the lumpy surfaces of airtight packages, patting sacks of jasmine rice, and marvelling at the diverse selection of noodle shapes. I recognize some greens my parents like to cook and try to read their labels in order to learn their Chinese names, but the words are completely incomprehensible to me. I can't even tell if it's supposed to be Mandarin, if I'm reading correctly, or if it's a matter of totally mistaking one vegetable name for another. We end up choosing a case of yogourt drinks and a bag of green grapes.

The line to the checkout follows the vertical side of the store, to the back, then around the bend. Emily and I look in old couples' baskets, taking turns guessing what they'll be cooking for dinner. Green onions, ginger, jars of Lǎo Gān Mā chili sauce. Tofu, stem lettuce, noodle packs, dark and light soy sauce, white shrimp, snow peas, radish.

"For lunch, they're serving soft tofu with a side of shrimp and soy sauce soup. For dinner: snow peas, just the shells. Very high in fibre."

When it's our turn to pay, I step up, breathe in, pause,

then squeak out a pathetic: "Credit, please." The āyí hands me my bag. I breathe in again, pause, and try harder: "Xiè xiè."

The āyí barely flicks her eyes at me, but I leave the store beaming.

"I thought I would come here and they would see I looked like them," I admit to Emily on our way out of the store.

There's a bakery at the end of Chinatown that will be closing soon because of rent increases, so many people are lining up outside to support the business one last time. Emily and I get in line to buy some buns to bring home.

Everyone in line is holding an orange plastic tray. I see a stack of them at the front of the bakery and take one as well. We select the buns we want and place them on our tray using tongs. We select two of everything, and I even pick up a container of overpriced almond cookies.

When I get up to pay, the cashier tells me in English that they only take cash. My face slumps, my limp arm still extended toward the cashier. Mandarin melts on my tongue like butter. Emily steps forward and hands the cashier a twenty from her wallet, but before I can thank her, two white people get up to pay and the procession continues until I'm pushed against the wall, hurriedly placing my card back in my wallet.

Emily doesn't want to go home yet, so we decide to see a movie. We walk from Chinatown to the theatre, and when we arrive, the movie we want to watch has already started playing. The lights have dimmed and it's difficult to find our way to our seats.

We seat ourselves as discreetly as we can, keeping our coats on. I'm trying to immerse myself in the moving screen, but I hear the crinkle of plastic next to me, followed by the sweet scent of custard. I prod Emily's knee until she passes me a bun.

We sit in the dark of the auditorium eating our buns. Crumbs fall onto the collar of my coat, down my chest. Emily laughs into the palm of her hand. She passes me another bun before I've even finished eating my first. Then she opens the plastic box of cookies with a loud crack. I lower my chin, stifling my laughter.

I'm not sure what the plot of the movie is supposed to be, but it's nice sitting in the dark with Emily. Bright flashes of colour dance across our faces. A mountain passes from her left cheek to her right, strokes of green and blue, from my left cheek to my right. Flowers blossom and rot.

I'm reminded of the time I went to see a movie with Johnny. It had been his idea to see a movie with subtitles, but before the movie was even over, he leaned over to me with complaints of a headache. The movie was about a little boy whose parents signed him up for piano lessons. The boy reminded me of myself. Short fused, stubborn, and easily distracted. He would rather listen to pop music on his MP3 player than sit for hours in front of the piano practising his scales. When his parents spoke to him in their native tongue, he would reply harshly in English. The boy only wanted to fit in with his classmates. He didn't want to learn classical music on the piano and be made fun of as even more of an Asian stereotype.

Not a single teacher wanted to teach this boy, so his parents had no choice but to ask the principal of the music institute if he would teach the boy himself. The principal was an elderly man who wore tweed suits with matching knit caps. He agreed to take the boy under his wing, but the boy still played his chords too quickly and used all the wrong fingering. Then, midway into their first year together, the principal fell ill, and the boy started seeing him less and less until, eventually, his lessons stopped altogether. When the boy found out that the principal had passed away, he said only one word, and he said it in his native tongue. "Grandpa!" the boy cried. That one word struck me in the heart.

Johnny thought the movie was just okay. I said nothing during the remainder of our date. It wasn't my intention to ignore him; I didn't know what to say, and he had nothing to say to me either.

The movie screen brightens, and I can see Emily's profile clearly.

Light leaks from the corners of my eyes; the theatre is like a glass sphere containing the entire universe, a glass dome filled with flecks of gold and trails of coloured glass.

04

I HAVE A MEMORY of walking with my mom behind the back of our apartment building. It's just her and me in the memory, and she was telling me a story about a little girl and her mom. She told me that, like many Chinese girls, the little girl in the story was at the top of her class and talented at playing instruments, but she was especially known for her skill with the pípá, which my mom explained was a traditional lute. A pear-shaped lute you cradle in your lap while plucking the strings.

优秀 (yōu xiù) is the adjective used to describe children like that: excellent students; outstanding; splendid; fine.

"That woman wanted to raise her only daughter to be perfect. Their story was in the news," my mom said. "Everyone knows it."

I can recall quite vividly the short grass lining both sides of the path. A few bright dandelions had sprouted during a night of rain. My mom had her hair up in a claw clip, the strands coming loose at the sides fringed by orange light.

"That is too much pressure to put on a child," my mom said, walking a few paces ahead of me. She was still wearing her maternity dress, even though she had already given birth to Emily. Wind seeped through the extra fabric of her dress, lifting her skirt like a soft, limp wing. I felt that her words were not spoken to me.

The girl's mom was aware of the pressure she was putting on her daughter. "If it's ever too much for you, tell me, and I will stop." Apparently, the woman said this because children were killing themselves all over China or something like that.

"I won't kill myself," her daughter promised.

One day, the girl, now grown, opened her bedroom window. She had a view of the concrete fountain below. It had rained all night and strong winds had blown many loose leaves into the fountain.

I didn't know why my mom was telling me this story. I was so young at the time. I walked beside her and listened seriously.

"Will you kill yourself too?" I remember my mom asking me this.

Her face was like a pond, the way it clouded over. Then she grabbed my hand and said, "Don't you ever grow up and stop talking to me. I will always try to understand you."

Before I could answer her, she sighed weakly and dropped my hand.

⁂

After Emily was born, something in me moved into the shade. It happened suddenly—Emily was born—outgoing, clever, empathetic, 优秀. I hid my face behind the trunks of trees, occasionally peering at her with one eye. Emily, who surpassed me in both mathematics and Mandarin, who opened her mouth and matched our dad's singing voice.

Emily, a daughter to be proud of.

I watched her walking between my parents, watched them hold her hand on each side like they had with me when it was just us three, the three of us living together in China. It would be the three of us forever; I would have been their only star.

To my parents, Emily represented the future. "So many years we've been away from home," they'd say. "But these have been years we've watched you grow."

Layer by layer, Emily thawed them. My parents yelled at each other less. They became more lenient. I watched Emily live her life with more freedom than I could even think to ask for. With all my worrying, I never could provide this respite for my parents.

To Emily, who was still in diapers at the time, our early days of poverty are only screen memories.

As for myself, sometimes in my memories of our apartment, I see a fountain below my window instead of a broken swing set.

Morning, and my mom stands facing her garden, waiting for the rain to end.

In the kitchen, there is no one else, just the sound of boiling water in a saucepan and three white eggs knocking softly into each other. My dad and Emily left together to go grocery shopping, so me and Mom have the house to ourselves.

Stepping toward her and clearing my throat so that she will not be surprised, I take the chair next to my mom and join her in waiting.

"Good, good," she mutters. "Drink up. Drink more. Grow big and strong."

She isn't looking at the garden; her vacant stare is fixed on the falling rain.

It is chilly enough in the house to make me shiver in my cotton robe. I wrap the sides of my robe tighter around myself. "When you were young—did you want—did you *even* want kids?"

She mulls over my question long enough for me to think she's dismissing me. Then, dove-like, she floats over to the stove and shuts the gas valve off with a flick of her wrist. After transferring the eggs into an ice bath, she rinses the saucepan and sets it aside to dry. She removes one egg from the water and rolls it between her palm and the kitchen counter until cracks form all over the shell; she repeats this with the remaining eggs, before peeling the shells into the compost.

"I cried when my ultrasound came back."

She places the eggs together in a bowl and brings the bowl to the table.

"I wanted twins. Your dad consoled me by saying, 'Everyone in China can only have one child—how many people would be lucky enough to have twins?'"

"I worried about you: Would you be healthy? Would you be beautiful? My only child. Some of the women I knew even framed photos of other peoples' babies that they thought were beautiful. They would walk around their apartments looking at these photos of strangers' babies, saying, 'I want my baby to look like that.'

"I never liked children. When I was in school every day they taught me about overpopulation, pollution. I was the person who sneered at women on the street walking with their kids. 'Stop having children!' I even heckled them. I was that way when I was young, so it surprised everyone when I wanted a second child.

"Since you can think to ask me a question like this, I can tell that you've grown up. I could always tell how sensitive a person you are. You are unlucky enough to have an insensitive mom like me. That's more reason I wanted you to have a sibling."

"How are you insensitive?" I ask. "What brings you to say things like that?"

"When you were born, I thought, *That's my life. I'm*

holding my own life in my arms. And I thought, *Ah, I will die.* I was so afraid thinking about how I will leave you alone one day. I never want you to be alone in this world.

"You've grown, Yuè Yuè. I can tell you worry about your dad and me. It's my fault your heart is tied to one place. I raised you and your sister with fear: Will you be happy? Will you survive in this cold country? Will you have enough to eat? I am too hard on you and not hard enough. Sometimes I think I don't know my daughters well at all, and I get depressed. Why am I so lazy that I don't try to improve my English? Why didn't I teach you more Chinese? Now I think it's too late—I look in the mirror and think, *Who is that old lady?*"

"You're not old. You're young."

"Don't cry. You haven't let me finish. Don't cry, listen. When I think like that, and I feel depressed, I see you and Emily talking with each other or reading together—the two of you are radiant—and life is good. Life has been good to me, to give me you two.

"That old lady in the mirror—the longer I look at her, the more I notice her eyes. She has such shiny black eyes.

"Her pupils are shiny and black, like longan seeds."

My mom swipes her thumb across my cheek tenderly.

"I gave you my eyes."

05

IN THE MIDDLE of the bed, there was a globe of snow. Inside the snow world, fairies came down from the mountains to bathe in the river. Peach trees grew along the water's edge, and during the early spring months, the surface of the water was covered in peach blossoms. When the peaches ripened and fell, deer and rabbits came to eat the fruit and rest in the shade.

Lodged in the roots of one tree was a woven basket. It simply appeared one morning as if by magic, so unexpected that even the fairies took it as a blessing.

想想看!

Imagine that!

"What could possibly surprise a fairy, who lives in delight every day of her life?" my mom asked.

I laid my head at the foot of the bed, watching the snow rise and fall with my mom's breathing. I had my ear against the blanket, and my mom's voice came to me muffled, as if in a dream.

Then I heard my dad saying, "You can't stay here."

你明天还要上学呢。

You still have school tomorrow.

My mom stopped telling her story. I inched forward on the bed until I could press my ear against that white globe. Mom lifted the blanket and the snow fell away in one great swoop. I pressed my ear to her hot belly and listened.

Dad was speaking to me from the door. He already had his coat on.

给你妈说个再见。

Say bye to your mom.

I pulled the blanket back over my mom's belly and once more pressed my face into the bed.

不要太娇气。

Don't be so dramatic.

让你妈休息。

Let your mom rest.

月月，啊，月月！别伤心！

Yuè Yuè, oh, Yuè Yuè! Don't be sad!

你明天回来就有妹妹了。

When you come back tomorrow, you will have a little sister.

I couldn't raise my head from the bed. I didn't want to keep my dad waiting, and I didn't want to keep my mom from resting, but I couldn't raise my head. My head felt like a big dumb rock stuck to the bed.

别伤心！伤心干吗？只是一天而已。你明天下了学就可以回来，你妈还会在这呢。

Don't be sad! Why are you sad? It's only for one day. You can come back after school tomorrow. Your mom will still be here.

The nurse came to check on my mom, and my dad stepped aside from the door to let her in. I quickly rose from the bed, but I couldn't keep the tears back the moment I lifted my face. They kept flowing and flowing. My eyes were still seeing those mountains, and that river, and all the snow from that world melted the second I returned to this one, so now I was like a river myself, flowing, flowing.

你为什么要这样呢? 来, 过来, 别哭了。告诉我们你为什么哭。

Why are you acting this way? Come, come here, don't cry. At least tell us what's wrong.

我不想说再见。

I don't want to say goodbye.

你总是那么极端。你明天还会见你妈的。

You are always too extreme. You will still see your mom tomorrow.

一转眼就是明天了。

In the blink of an eye, it will be tomorrow.

我不想要时间走。

I don't want time to pass.

我不想说再见。

I don't want to say goodbye.

The nurse walked past me to my mom. My dad led me down the hall without a word. I cried quietly because I felt bad for not saying bye and because I felt bad for how loud I had been crying.

When my dad picked me up after school the next day, he was smiling.

你记得, 月月。

Remember, Yuè Yuè.

有改变是好事。

Change is good.

Dad took me to the hospital. We took the elevator up to the sixth floor and walked down the hall into the room where we had been the previous night. Everything was the same. Beige curtains opened in the middle to let in a bit of light, a blue armchair in the corner by the heater, a single bed.

My dad pointed to the bed and said:

看!

Look!

There she was: my mom, and my sister.

Acknowledgments

A chapter from this novel appeared in *Room* magazine's Issue 44.4 as "Lǐ Zhī's House"—thank you, Selina Boan, for soliciting my work.

Thank you, Professor Uzoma Esonwanne, for introducing me to the theory of repetition. Thank you especially to my mentor, Anne Michaels, and my creative writing cohort: Andalah, Masha, Anna, Marina, Tyler, Kara, Jordan. What was once transparent like onion skin has finally taken shape!

Thank you Canadian Encyclopedia on ducks and Pleco Chinese Dictionary.

Thank you to my editor, Shirarose Wilensky. Your care and precision inspire me endlessly.

Alyson, Tasneem, Anita. Thank you for believing in the first draft. Thank you to Mimi for the translation help. To all my friends who accept me and support me: I hold your kind words and gestures in my heart always!

Finally, to my dear sisters and parents: every word I dedicate to you.

About the Author

LILY WANG (they/them) was born in Shanghai in 1997 and moved to Canada in 2004. The author of the poetry collection *Saturn Peach*, they have an MA in English and Creative Writing from the University of Toronto.

Publishing in the Public Interest

Thank you for reading this book published by The New Press; we hope you enjoyed it. New Press books and authors play a crucial role in sparking conversations about the key political and social issues of our day.

We hope that you will stay in touch with us. Here are a few ways to keep up to date with our books, events, and the issues we cover:

- Sign up at www.thenewpress.com/subscribe to receive updates on New Press authors and issues and to be notified about local events
- www.facebook.com/newpressbooks
- www.twitter.com/thenewpress
- www.instagram.com/thenewpress

Please consider buying New Press books not only for yourself, but also for friends and family and to donate to schools, libraries, community centers, prison libraries, and other organizations involved with the issues our authors write about.

The New Press is a 501(c)(3) nonprofit organization; if you wish to support our work with a tax-deductible gift please visit www.thenewpress.com/donate or use the QR code below.